BETRAYAL

A. MARIE

CONTENTS

© *2020 Ashley Tillman*

ISBN# 978-1-7350337-0-9

LCCN# 2020907912

☐

*S*MACK.

Leah hit the floor, hard with tears in her eyes.

"What the fuck was that for Marcus?" she said as she looked up at him in confusion.

"Bitch you and that fly ass mouth of yours, you always got some slick shit to say," he barked as he paced the floor back and forth.

"So, you mean to tell me you're mad at me for catching you with a bopper's lips wrapped around your little black dick, I confront you about it and now I'm the one in the wrong here?" She shouted.

The fucking nerve of him, trying to turn this shit around on me, she thought as she stood and held her face from the sting of his hand. This mufucka had lost his mind with the manipulation game and now Leah was about to lose hers as well because she was tired of enduring being beat on by this punk ass nigga. Baby daddy or not Marcus was about to catch her hands. She didn't care if she couldn't whoop him, she was going to attempt to give him a run for his money. Leah stood up, looked him square in the eyes and spit directly in his face.

Marcus grimaced as he swiped a hand down his face, instantly growing heated. "You nasty bitch," he barked with a malicious look on his face. Leah had never disrespected him in such a way. And today was the day this abusive boy, because he wasn't a man would feel her fucking pain. Leah punched him dead in the nose and kicked him right in the dick.

"Agh," Marcus yelled out in agony.

He instantly dropped to his knees from the strong force behind the kick she had just delivered.

"Yeah, nigga some of that," she spat as he hollered in pain.

Leah was tired of the bullshit. Every time she turned around it was different tramps texting and calling his phone. Marcus was a cheating ass nigga and Leah was tired of it. She was beyond fed the fuck up with the fighting and the disrespectful words he used when speaking to her. Here she was only 19, with a baby on the way with an abusive child's father.

Leah wanted a better life for her and her unborn daughter. Being with Marcus caused her both love and pain however, the pain he caused outweighed the love he gave. She had been with Marcus for the last 8 months and she was tired of living life according to him and how he thought she should be. Her self-esteem was at an all-time low, she didn't even consider herself beautiful anymore because he had stripped her of that. When she looked at herself in the mirror, she no longer saw beauty or the girl she used to be. What she saw staring back at her was a young woman with black eyes, with green and blue bruises that covered her body. Leah darted from the house, she needed to get away from the drama. She climbed inside her god mom's truck that sat in the driveway

2

and sobbed. The amount of emotions that flowed from her was heart wrenching. Leah rested her head on the red fuzzy steering wheel as she wondered how her life had taken a turn for   the   worse.

CHAPTER ONE

☐

Summer of 2001

$\mathcal{I}$t was the end of Leah's Junior year in high school, she had just turned 18 a few months before. As the end of the school year and summer break approached, Leah was very anxious to be entering into her senior year, it would be her last year in high school and she wanted to enjoy this last year by all means necessary. Leah was beautiful, with soft caramel skin, slightly slanted dark brown eyes with a slim and curvy waistline. The song *Bootylicious* by Destiny's Child should have been made for her because for her to be small in the waist she had an ass on her.

Leah rocked with only two girls throughout her entire high school years. Mandy and NuNu. They were her riders, right or wrong, they had her back. She had known NuNu since 5th grade and she had met Mandy their 9th grade year because all three of them shared the same 1st hour. Leah had asked to borrow a pen and then NuNu needed one as well. All three girls shared a laugh after Mandy said. "Damn, I see none of you hoes came prepared." Leah knew then that she would fit right in because they all had the same attitude and didn't care what came out of their mouth. Since that day they have been inseparable. When you saw one, better believe the other two weren't far behind. And for summer break they had big plans. They were ready to fuck some shit up, straight kick it before they had to buckle down and truly focus on their Senior year and graduation.

Leah, Mandy, and NuNu had linked up after the last day of school and were walking down Hamilton Street on the south side of Toledo. They were heading to Hamilton Park where everyone they knew would be posted up. The sun was out and the sky was clear. An absolutely beautiful day. The boys were playing basketball and the girls loved to watch. Leah wore a blue bleached skirt and a red half button down top that was sleeveless and revealed her stomach slightly. Leah wasn't privileged, at all, so her fashion came from the hood stores like *Dots* or *Fashion Cents*. Though her threads weren't costly, you still couldn't tell her shit, she could piece some fabrics together and make it look as if it cost a pretty penny. She was effortlessly pretty no matter what she wore, and she knew for a fact that she was the shit. Conceited. Leah was definitely conceited but let her tell it she was simply laced with confidence.

Leah saw her teenage love sitting on the hood of his 1986 grey Cutlass ride. Mike Jones, *Dick Don't Fail Me Now* was pouring out of his speakers while his homies engaged in a game of *Blackjack* in front of his car. Leah being the goofy friend out of the three girls, started snapping her fingers while doing hip rolls and other little dance gestures as they walked past the boys. The girls laughed as they went to cross over to the other side of the street. The boy watched Leah as she passed by. *Damn, who is that?* He thought. That's when he stopped her, he was standing there wearing an all grey valor Jordan sweat suit, with grey and white retro number 9 Jordan's to match. He was chocolate with thick bushy eyebrows, light brown eyes, full lips and a posture so damn enticing that he made even ladies much older than him swoon. Leah couldn't help but stop and be caught in his trance. She stared at him as he stared back, until he finally broke the silence between them.

"What's up bey?" Marcus asked as he grinned slightly.

Leah bit into her bottom lip and batted her eyes up at him.

Damn, he is fine as hell, she thought to herself.

"I don't know, you tell me, *bey* since you're the one that grabbed me and pulled me over here to you." She replied with a grin.

"What's your name baby girl?" he asked as he stared into her eyes.

He was drawn to her, the way she bit into her pink bottom lip sent a spark down to his little man. Her aura was different from what he was familiar with, and he couldn't make sense of the instant attraction he had. Even the soft baby hairs that she had as sideburns attracted him. She was just pretty as hell to him.

"Leah," she replied sweetly.

Marcus licked his chocolate lips and started to speak again before he was interrupted by his boys arguing over the card game.

"Nigga we said double the bet, the fuck you mean?" his homie City said.

6

"Bitch nigga that was our last bet. We went back to our normal shits, the fuck you talking about?" his other dude Shan Shan spat back.

"Y'all mufuckas chill damn," Marcus yelled.

"Man, Marcus this nigga always on some goofy shit." City spat.

His boys were forever arguing over something while gambling. Them and gambling with money just didn't mix. In fact, they hardly ever got along but outside niggas wouldn't know because they were brothers and would rock anybody over one another.

"Hold on baby, give me a second let me get these niggas in line," he stated to Leah before removing her from in front of him. Leah waited while Marcus talked to his boys.

"*Marcus,*" she said to herself after overhearing his name.

Leah smiled as she said his name again this time in her head. NuNu stepped up to her with impatience. She wasn't with standing around watching Leah dote over Marcus. She was ready to go and didn't have any shame in expressing it.

"Damn, girl what are we waiting for?" she asked, slightly annoyed.

Leah turned to her, poked both lips out and tilted her head to the side.

"Girl you just trying to get down to Hamilton Park to see Tyson big head ass you not slick," she replied, shaking her head.

Mandy busted out laughing because she too knew that was why NuNu was being impatient. NuNu couldn't contain her smile, "so what y'all know I don't want to miss his fine ass running up and down the court," she said. All Leah could

7

do was continue shaking her head because she had known when it came to the three of them going to the park, NuNu had one mission. Getting to Tyson.

He wasn't from their city and NuNu had been crushing on him for months. Leah knew her friend had a desire to lay eyes on the east coast boy that had come to their city hustling low-key. The girls started walking off heading toward their destination. Marcus was still talking with his boys and Leah didn't care to wait much longer. Just before Leah could get too far Marcus called for her.

"Hold up baby," he said motioning for her with his hand to come back.

Leah turned back to her girls with pleading eyes. She really wanted to talk to him. She also knew that NuNu wanted to talk to Tyson.

"Y'all let me see what he wants real quick, just give me 5 mins and I promise we can roll after that."

Mandy nodded and Leah beelined back to Marcus. NuNu rolled her eyes and caught an attitude, she wasn't trying to waste any more time waiting on Leah. *Shit I got my own nigga I want to talk to*, she thought. Tyson wasn't hers but she was speaking it into existence. She had convinced Mandy that they should just keep walking, leaving Leah behind. Leah was so caught up in what Marcus wanted, she didn't even notice when her girls left her standing there.

Marcus took her by the hand and led her to his car. "Rap with me for a minute bey," he requested as he opened the passenger side door for her. Leah climbed in without hesitation, instantly getting comfortable as the bass from his music vibrated throughout her chest. Marcus quickly ran around to the driver's side and hopped in. He turned the radio down and just looked at her. *This girl is so fucking pretty*, he thought once more. Marcus was fascinated by the way she looked. As he observed her, he realized she wasn't like other girls around the hood. She had a uniqueness about her that made her stand out from others. Leah noticed his stare and grew nervous as she played with the gold *L* ring that she wore on her right hand. Noticing her discomfort, he finally spoke.

"Ah, bey you can relax. Don't be nervous," he said reaching across the center console, stopping her from fidgeting with her ring. Leah looked out her window and he guided her face back towards him.

"So how old are you Leah?" Marcus quizzed.

"I just turned 18 a few months back," she replied.

"Oh yeah, that's what's up, I'm 20," Marcus stated as he continued with more questions. "What school do you go to?"

"I'm a junior at Libbey," she replied.

Marcus laughed.

"Oh, so you repping them cowgirls?" he stated, mocking her school's mascot, the Cowboys.

Leah shot him a piercing look then laughed.

"Don't even go there homie, you must be a Bullfrog?" She said, mocking his right back. Libbey and Scott were rival high schools and by him saying cowgirls, she knew he attended Scott since that's how the two schools addressed one another. Marcus laughed hard and shook his head.

"I used to attend Scott, but I dropped out and started chasing my paper."

"You couldn't chase paper and go to school?" she asked, her eyes penetrating his.

He looked at her for a moment. *Damn, she's picking at my brain right now*, he thought. Marcus examined every inch of her before diverting away from the question, asking her to ride with him while they chopped it up. Without even thinking twice she nodded her head in compliance. Marcus stuck his head out of his window and yelled, "yo, City and Shan Shan get from in front of my shit, I'm leaving." They approached the car, dapped him up, and headed to their own cars that were parked in Shan Shan's driveway. The boys were stick up kids, dope boys, and getting to the money. Old school cars and 20-inch custom rims were the life for them. Marcus's OG had put him in the game when he was only 15. He had dropped out of high school and had run the north side of his city ever since. Marcus had met City and Shan Shan while making moves on the south side of Toledo and the three just clicked. They were all after the same things, money, cars, clothes, and girls.

Marcus pulled from the curb and told Leah to DJ.

"I don't think you want me to do that, all I really listen to is old school slow jams homie," she said.

"Try me," he chuckled.

Leah reached for the cd case that was on the floor at her feet. She flipped through it and to her surprise Marcus had quite the collection of R&B music. "I never would have thought you'd be into slow jams," she said as she popped in Roger and played, *I Want to Be Your Man*. Marcus smirked as she began to sing the words to the song. Leah noticed and stopped singing; she was embarrassed.

"No, please keep going," he stated as he cut the music down so he could hear her a little better.

She blushed and shook her head, declining to continue. This boy had her flustered, her heart raced, and she went right back to fidgeting with the ring on her finger.

"What do you know about some Roger anyway bey?" He asked, smiling as he steered with one hand and reached for her hand with the other. He gave her a gentle squeeze, that was so comforting Leah melted a little.

"With an old school dad, I know a lot baby," she replied, finally looking at him, shooting him a wink.

Marcus was driving nowhere in particular until he found himself getting ready to ride past Walbridge park. The park was the perfect place for them to be able to walk and talk. It ran alongside the Maumee River and the scenery was beautiful. "So how are you 18 and still a junior?" he asked as he pulled over into the parking lot of the park.

"Boy don't act like you never flunked a grade before," she said laughing.

"Aight, my fault you right, I think we all probably failed 1st or 2nd grade," he said maneuvering into a spot and killing the engine.

"Right, so act like you know," she said as she climbed out of the car.

Marcus climbed out the car as well and approached her, looping his arm through hers as they started to walk. Leah breathed in deep. The air was refreshing. Being on Marcus's arm was calming. A walk in the park with a fine boy is something she had never experienced and she was enjoying the moment. Leah and Marcus walked around the park for at

11

least two hours talking about any and everything that came to mind down to the most trivial things such as their favorite foods and colors. She noticed the smallest things about him down to the way he walked. He was pigeon toed and she thought it was the sexiest shit ever.

Neither Leah nor Marcus could deny their intense chemistry. With these feelings Leah knew this was just the beginning of something, she just wasn't sure what was in store.

CHAPTER TWO

☐

*N*uNu sat on top of the picnic tables as she and Mandy watched the group of boys run up and down the basketball court. She couldn't keep her eyes off Tyson as he shook his opponents on the court. His tattooed covered body was shirtless, and he wore black Jordan basketball shorts with all black Jordan retro 13s to match. She wanted to beat his ass for showing off his body. *All these hoes bopping around here*, she thought to herself. She couldn't understand why she was so jealous. Tyson wasn't her man, hell she had never uttered a word to him, but she couldn't help the attraction she had for him. NuNu wanted him to be hers, she wanted him to pay attention to her in the way she paid attention to him. *He never seems to notice me*, she reflected as she continued to watch him like a hawk. Her eyes roamed his entire body and she couldn't help but notice his dick bouncing every time he went up to take a shot. NuNu's entire clit started to pulse when he hit a jump shot at the right angle and if she saw that shit, she knew them hoes seen it as well. She was livid at the thought but at the same time, she couldn't stop the freaky thoughts going through her mind. She wanted him in every way possible.

NuNu had a mission today, she was so eager to get to the park before Leah's ass insisted on stopping to talk to that

13

nigga Marcus. She had finally built up the courage to approach Tyson and ask for his number. That was her mission. Her main goal. And she was dead set on accomplishing it by all means necessary.

Once the boys were done playing, Tyson began strolling over to the picnic table where NuNu was sitting. His Nike gym bag sat on the ground right next to her. NuNu's heart felt like it was beating out of her chest when she noticed him coming her way.

"Oh my god girl here he comes," she said to Mandy who didn't seem to be paying attention because she was too busy texting and playing snake on her new Nokia phone.

Mandy just shook her head and smiled. She noticed NuNu getting nervous.

"Don't act all scary now tramp, you've been wanting to talk to him all day and now here's your chance," she said as Tyson slapped hands with one of his boys and then finally approached the table.

Oh shit. NuNu thought when he finally stood next to her reaching inside the gym bag for his towel. She just sat there gawking. Tyson wiped his face and then threw the towel over his shoulder. Once he caught her stare, he winked at her. NuNu thought she would fucking faint as she reached for Mandy's arm. She released a harsh breath and smiled at him as he zipped his bag and started to walk away. She called to him.

"Um, Tyson wait."

She stood up as he halted and waited for her to walk toward him.

"What it do ma?" He asked.

Again, NuNu felt as if she would faint. *This boy is fucking fine,* she thought as she took him in. She had fucked him 3 times in her head already and was hooked, that's how fine he was. Yeah, she had it bad and she knew it.

Tyson was from the east coast and had moved to Toledo to finally be with his mother after living with his uncle. He stood 5'8, he wasn't too tall or too short. His light skin was flawless. His brown eyes were enticing. Lips soft like pillows and just as pink as the penny candy NuNu would get from the corner stores. His wavy hair was spinning so hard it made NuNu dizzy, but that fucking beard is what made him stand out. Dudes from Toledo were rocking baby faces and here came this east coast nigga switching shit up that would for sure set a trend. God, she wanted to kiss him right here and right now cause the sight of him had her body igniting. Shit, she wanted to thank his mama for creating such a fine ass specimen. Tyson snapped his fingers snapping her out of her thoughts.

"What's up ma? You just zoned out."

NuNu shook her head as she came out of the fantasy in her head. She'd be sure to thank his mama later, because there was no way she was leaving this park without his number. She grew nervous as hell as she tried to gather words that wouldn't make her seem pressed like the other girls that tried to get Tyson to notice them. They all bopped around half naked, trying way too hard for the attention that he clearly wasn't giving. To him, they were just like the skuzzies back home and he didn't have an itch for those types.

"Um, Tyson I don't know if you noticed or whatever, but I really like you, I mean *really* like you. I've been observing you for a little over 6 months but never said anything because I wanted you to notice me first." She could barely look him in the eye because she was so damn nervous. *Why am I so damn nervous? I'm the most outspoken out of the three of us and here I am barely able to look this boy in the eyes*, she thought. It didn't help that he kept licking them pink ass lips of his while she fumbled over her words. Tyson reached out and grabbed her chin, making NuNu weak in the knees just from his firm but soft touch. If she didn't understand what SWV meant in their song *Weak*, she knew now. Tyson had her weak in the knees and she could hardly speak.

"I noticed you ma," he stated as he looked at her. "The crazy thing is I never said anything because I just knew you would chase me like these other skuzzies do, but you didn't and that intrigued me." He continued, "I watched while you were with the little dark skin nigga and then after." NuNu couldn't contain the smile that spread across her face. She looked down at her feet and then twirled her ring with the letter *N* on it. She and Leah had got them at the same time and just like her friend when she grew nervous, she played with it. Tyson lifted her chin again, "I had my eyes on you down in Florida as well at the tournament. You were finer than a mufucka in that orange swimsuit *lor mama*, I was going to step to you, but you beat me to it," he chuckled.

NuNu couldn't believe what she was hearing. He was admitting that he had noticed her after all. She smiled.

"I didn't want to seem like these other chicks but I could no longer take not being able to get to know you so that's why I'm standing here now wanting your number so we can talk," she replied shyly. She immediately went back to fiddling with the ring. She couldn't understand why he made her feel so uneasy.

Tyson took her hand. He had noticed how he made her nervous and thought it was sexy. He added that to the list of characteristics that she had and that he adored.

"Relax ma," he said as he guided her toward his all red 1989 Regal that sat on spoked rims. His uncle had put him in a position to make money with his mom's new boyfriend and he was killing it on the blocks. His uncle taught him how to move smart, so he always stayed low-key. The only thing that made him stand out from the rest was his swag. It was different. He was different.

Before opening her door, he paused "How about we head to my place and talk there and before I drop you off at home, I'll give you my number," he said as he reached out and caressed her cheek. NuNu's body started heating from his touch. She was timid and wanted to say no. She hadn't expected him to be this game, but she couldn't, she wouldn't turn down his offer either. *I'd be a damn fool to tell him no,* she thought to herself. She nodded in response and Tyson pulled open his passenger door.

"So, I'm meeting your moms already?"

Tyson cracked a wide grin.

"Push down on them breaks baby girl, I didn't say all that," he said, licking his lips.

Those damn lips. She wanted to caress them with her tongue, that's how good they looked. They were now NuNu's favorite part of his face.

17

"Let's see how things go first and *if* it's meant to play out like that, you'll be the first and only one to meet my dukes."

Tyson had never been the type to take girls to meet his mother. If they were only going to be in his life for a season, there was no need for them to meet the woman who gave him life. That was something he was going to reserve for his future wife. The girl he was certain that was not going to be temporary in his life. With NuNu, he had a feeling that she would actually end up being that one. The one who wouldn't be temporary and worthy of meeting the woman who made him into the man he was. The attraction he had for her was magnetic, he had felt it as soon as she spoke to him.

NuNu smiled, finally climbing in the car but popped right back out yelling for Mandy. "Aye, Mandy you okay? Do you mind?"

Mandy climbed down off the picnic table dusted her butt off and walked towards her.

"Yeah I mind," she said with a wink as she reached in and hugged NuNu.

"About time yo ass stopped being scary and you bet not fuck him on the first date," she whispered. The girls shared a laugh and then agreed to get with one another again before the day was over.

Mandy headed back in the opposite direction she had other things to attend to anyway, she just wanted to support her friend with her silly mission. NuNu climbed in the car and leaned her head against the headrest and all she could think about is not fucking this nigga. She was a virgin, but it was just something about this boy that made her want to pop it for him. She had come close to having sex with her ex-boyfriend Dominic, but she couldn't will herself to do it, she just didn't feel like he was the right one and because of that, they broke up. He wanted to take their relationship to the next level, but she wasn't ready.

"Lord, please let me keep my self-discipline please, please," she uttered to herself. Tyson climbed into the car and asked her if she was good. Again, NuNu nodded because now all of a sudden, her vocabulary was gone. Tyson smiled as he sensed her nervousness and held out a hand for her to take. She did and he held onto her the entire drive to his house, while they listened to Ja Rule and Charlie Baltimore's collabo *Down Ass Chick* bumping through his stereo. All NuNu could think about was being Tyson's *down ass chick*. She wanted to be the chick that would be down for him no matter what. She had made up her mind that she was going to be just that.

Tyson and NuNu entered his home and she looked around impressed by the lavishness of his home. From the outside, you would never be able to tell that it looked so beautiful on the inside. *Never judge a book by its cover,* she thought to herself.

"Do I need to remove my shoes?" NuNu asked before taking a step further inside.

"As long as your feet don't stink baby girl, be my guest," Tyson said playfully.

NuNu punched him in the arm as she smirked.

"My feet don't stink homie," she said as she kicked her shoes off. Her feet immediately sunk into the plush carpet.

Tyson laughed. "Have a seat Ma, I'm about to hop in the shower real quick," he said as he headed toward the back room. NuNu took a seat in the reclining chair and began getting comfortable as she waited. She looked up noticing pictures of Tyson sitting on top of the beautifully decorated mantle. She stood from her seat and tip toed toward it as she peeked down the hall to make sure he didn't catch her looking around.

Tyson had to be the only child because the mantle was aligned with pictures of only him from a baby until he was 18 it seemed. NuNu noticed a picture of him in the swimming pool as a young boy with a basketball in his hand. She smiled at the sight of that. NuNu went down the entire row of pictures, admiring them. "He was a cute kid", she said to herself as she came across his graduation picture. She picked the picture up and caressed it, "Gosh this boy is fucking fine," she whispered. Tyson had emerged from the backroom freshly showered, smelling like *Cool Water* cologne with nothing but basketball shorts and a white beater on. Noticing NuNu admiring his pictures, he crept up on her wrapping his arms around her waist and then squeezed her gently. NuNu jumped in surprise and spun around, she was getting ready to haul off and hit him until she saw him biting into his bottom lip, smiling at her and just like that, she was caught in his spell. *Damn, he smells good.*

"Did I scare you Ma?"

The way NuNu was acting you would have thought she had been hit by cupid himself.

"No," she said.

They took a seat on the couch and Tyson turned the tv on and an old episode of Martin was playing.

"This my show," NuNu said as she turned, placing her feet in Tyson's lap.

"I see you're comfortable now and not all nervous," he said with a smirk.

NuNu was, in fact, comfortable in his space, with his presence, and she couldn't believe it. The attraction she was feeling with him was refreshing... it was... it was relaxing. She smiled as she looked over to him.

"I am." She replied. "Tell me why you stayed back home with your uncle? I meant to ask you on the way here," she quizzed.

"Dukes moved here my junior year with her man, but I wanted to stay in B-More to finish high school. So, my uncle said I could stay with him until I was finished but I ended up staying longer to make money," he explained.

Tyson removed her feet from his lap and opened her legs as he climbed in between them. NuNu just sat there as she anticipated things to move quicker than she expected. Her heart was racing, and her breaths became slow. *Girl you better not let this suave man go any further, keep some self-discipline, keep some self fucking discipline*, she thought coaching herself. NuNu closed her eyes and breathed deep as she tried to find the words to stop him. Tyson being able to read her mind leaned in and pecked her lips. NuNu eyes popped back open. Tyson smiled.

"Don't worry *lor mama*, I'm not that type of cat when it comes to you," he said.

He was mesmerized by her beauty. He studied her face as he took her in. NuNu had his heart pumping differently. She had him on some first love type shit. The chic's back home

21

couldn't compare to this Toledo chic laying before him. NuNu was a rare breed. She was angelic and he wanted to be the only one to claim her from this day forward. So, for her, Tyson planned to move differently.

"Your body I can wait for, we just chilling," he said as he laid in between her thighs and got comfortable.

NuNu looked down at his head in stun. Her panties were getting moist because this man was impressing the hell out of her. If he kept this talk up, she would be losing all restraint. The way he was talking had her ready to pop pussy on the first date and not think twice about it. NuNu took a deep breath.

"Tyson, I don't trust myself with you," she whispered as she rubbed the top of his wavy head.

"I don't trust myself with you *lor mama*."

They laid on the couch talking and watching old episodes of Martin until eventually night fell and exhaustion took over them   both.

CHAPTER THREE

☐

*M*andy finally made it home from the park. A short dark-skinned boy sat on her porch with a pen and notepad writing, she walked up to him smiling. He looked up from what he was doing, putting his stuff down and Mandy immediately fell into his embrace and hugged him tightly.

"What took you so long baby?" Dominic asked, pecking her lips.

Mandy looked at him as if he should have already known but instead of getting annoyed with his question she simply replied, "I had to wait for NuNu to leave the park, I didn't want to seem like I was in a rush because then she would have been asking me what I was getting into that had me wanting to leave so soon." He took a seat back on the porch sitting her down in between his legs and draped his arms over her shoulders.

"Why don't you just tell her the truth?" he asked.

Mandy shook her head.

"Are you fucking crazy Nic? She would beat my ass. You're her ex and now I'm fucking you and smiling in her face every day."

"Well, she should have appreciated me when we were together, and she wouldn't have a reason to be upset."

Mandy shook her head at his stupid response. *Who the fuck do this nigga think he is?* She thought. "Let me ask you this, why don't we both just tell her...together?" Dominic got up from behind her, walked down the steps and stood directly in front of her. Mandy looked his short ass dead in the eyes and waited for his lame excuse on why they just couldn't tell NuNu about how they had been sneaking behind her back fucking for months since the night she and Dominic broke up.

Mandy knew this thing between them was dead wrong, smutty but yet here she was in love with one of her best friend's ex-man and she felt immoral about it. NuNu and Leah were her best friends and she knew the friendship would surely end once her truth was revealed. Dominic had started speaking but Mandy was doing everything except paying attention. Her mind was racing, thinking about how she ended up in this sticky web of love and deceit.

NuNu called Mandy crying at 1:30 in the morning on a Saturday. She and Dominic had just got back from a date at the movies. Scary Movie 3 which was a comedy remake of the movie Scream had just come out and NuNu had wanted to see the movie because she loved the character Brenda from the previous 2 movies. After the movies, they went to NuNu's place which they had to themselves since her mother was out of town for the weekend with her boyfriend. NuNu had no younger siblings being that she was the baby out of her mother's three children, so she had all the privacy in the world this weekend.

NuNu and Dominic sat on the living room couch once they kicked off their shoes. Even though there was no carpet

24

throughout the house, her mother still didn't allow people to wear shoes inside. Before NuNu got too comfortable, she asked if Dominic wanted anything to drink on her way to the kitchen to get herself a bottle of water. He declined.

They sat there laughing and talking about their favorite parts of the movie as NuNu got comfortable, kicking her feet up on Dominic's lap allowing him to rub them. "Brenda so ghetto," NuNu said laughing as she took a sip from the Dasani water bottle. Dominic laughed as well as he agreed with her adding his own comments regarding some of the other characters. The way he was rubbing her feet while they talked was relaxing her entire body.

"You know you give the best rubs Nic Nic," she stated as she laughed.

She knew he hated it when she called him that. Dominic smacked his lips and shook his head. "Man, NuNu don't start that Nic Nic stuff with me," he said to her.

She laughed again, leaning forward to peck his lips. He pulled back and she smiled, pecking his lips again, forcing him to finally give into her.

"You know I hate that name and yo ass always want to be funny."

"I know you hate it but I'm going to call you that whenever I please," she said.

Their pecking had turned into actual kissing now and Dominic's hands started to roam her body. NuNu leaned back while bringing him with her so that he was directly on top of her. Dominic's manhood started to grow hard and NuNu's body started reacting. He slid a hand up her shirt and popped her right breast out of her bra. Once he realized she wasn't stopping him he lowered his lips to her erect nipple and started licking it softly, making NuNu moan softly. He circled her nipple slowly with his tongue and then picked up the pace. She was responding to his touch exactly how he wanted her to, so he tried his luck and slid his hands down to her pants and unbuttoned them making it easier for him to be able to access her hidden treasure.

They had been dating for 5 months. NuNu wasn't the type of girl that would just give her body away. It was her temple. Her most prized possession and she took pride in being able to say she was still a virgin at 18.

By letting Dominic go this far had him thinking he was finally about to have sex with the second girl he ever dated. He continued his journey of four play and his hand finally dipped into her panties. He could feel how swollen her womanhood was and noticed that it was bare except for a trail of soft hair right down the middle. NuNu moaned as he played with her. She was into it at the moment and thought she was ready. He tried to enter a finger inside her and she tensed and grew uncomfortable. "Wait, Nic that hurts," she said as she pulled at his arm. He was so excited that he was barely paying attention to her body language. He didn't even pay attention to her tone nor did he pay attention to her discomfort.

"Damn Nu what the fuck?!" He said as he instantly became frustrated at her lack of cooperation all of sudden.

"You can gone with the attitude Nic, I told you it hurts, and you didn't listen. I refuse to let you enter me in any way for your own pleasure. That shit is just not about to happen."

26

Dominic sat all the way up in complete irritation and abruptly stood. He looked down at her as she started zipping her pants back up and adjusting her clothes.

"NuNu, I'm tired of fucking playing with you man. It's been 5 long damn months of us dry humping and fucking kissing I'm ready for something else. I'm ready for more and you're playing,"

She looked up at him with the craziest look on her face. She laughed.

"Are you fucking serious right now?" She asked.

"Serious as fuck," he said angrily.

"Like I said, man, we been at the shit for 5 months and I'm tired of fucking playing with you and I'm tired of leaving with blue balls all because your ass acting like you scared of dick."

NuNu couldn't believe what she was hearing, Dominic was acting as if he was truly after what was between her legs and could care less about her heart. Tears instantly started to fall from her eyes as she stood and then slapped the fuck out of him.

"How dare you talk to me like that as if my feelings don't matter?" She screamed.

Dominic held his face and then smirked.

"Look if we not fucking, I'm leaving and this childish ass relationship you got me in is fucking over." He said boldly.

That earned his ass another slap to the other side followed by a punch in the chest. NuNu was aggressive when she was angry or when her feelings were hurt. She was not only the baby of the family, but she was the only girl growing up with two older brothers that had made sure she was able to fight rather if it was male or female. *That punch had pissed Dominic off and instead of him hitting her ass back like he really wanted to, he called her a "bitch" and headed for the front door. He slipped his shoes on and pulled the door open. NuNu followed behind him while yelling that it was over and that she was done was his dawg ass. Dominic always was quick with his responses and shot back, "bitch I was just going to hit and quit it anyways," slamming the door as he made his exit.*

NuNu stood there with her mouth wide open, tears falling and heart completely hurting. She couldn't believe what had just gone down and how her relationship just ended in such a crazy way. She ran to her purse and pulled out her phone dialing up Mandy. As the phone rang, she paced back and forth as she waited impatiently for Mandy to answer. When her best friend picked up the tears started falling heavier as she tried to speak. Mandy immediately alarmed spoke in the phone loudly, "Nu what's wrong what's wrong?" NuNu's chest rose up and down as she cried but still couldn't get her words out. Mandy clicked over and dialed Leah. Leah answered on the first ring.

"What's up Mandy? It's late."

"It's Nu, she is on the other end crying and I can't get her to talk I'm about to click you in and hopefully you can get it out of her." Mandy merged the lines as Leah heard,

"He, he, he played me for a foooool."

"Nu, what's going on? You have to calm down and talk to us baby," Leah said, cutting her off.

NuNu took a deep breath and tried to calm herself. Leah was the best friend that was calm and nurturing. She always

28

was able to calm NuNu and get her to relax. NuNu was catching a slight headache from how hard she was crying. *"Matter of fact, I'm coming down there Nu. I'll be there in 10 let me put some clothes on real quick and then I'll be right there."* Leah disconnected from the girl's three-way call and Mandy remained on the line.

"Nu what happened between you and Nic? Y'all just had a date today and I thought everything was fine."

NuNu slid down to the floor and put her back against the front door, sighing.

"Yeah, we did, and our day was perfect overall Man," she replied.

"Well, what happened?" Mandy pushed.

A tear slid down NuNu's face and she swiped it away as she started telling Mandy what happened. *"We went to dinner and then the movies, after the movies we came back here and started talking about the movie. We started kissing and…"*

Knock Knock

"Hold on Man I think this is Leah."

NuNu got up from the floor while balancing her phone between her cheek and shoulder and turned toward the door. She opened it and Leah came walking in, pulling NuNu into a hug. NuNu dropped her phone as she hugged Leah tight and began to cry again. Leah pulled back wiping NuNu's face, kicking off her shoes because she knew Ms. Drea didn't play about shoes being worn in her house, and started leading NuNu to the couch. The girls began talking about what happened. NuNu had completely forgotten about Mandy being on the phone as she told Leah what happened.

29

Mandy remained on the line as she listened to how she and Dominic were about to have sex but NuNu had become uncomfortable and couldn't go through with the act. She heard NuNu tell Leah how Dominic didn't take the signs, that his touch was getting aggressive because he was so excited. When she heard that he told NuNu that he was going to hit and quit it she hung up and dialed Dominic's sister. Mandy and his sister shared the same World Studies class, so they often exchanged notes and helped each other with homework.

The phone rang twice, and Dominic's sister picked up.

"Hello," DaShay said, answering the phone.

"Is Dominic there?" Mandy asked.

"Oh, hey Mandy, yeah he's here." She said recognizing Mandy's voice, confused why she was calling this late for her brother. However, it wasn't her business, so she called for him and handed over the phone. Dominic taking the phone looked at the caller ID and didn't recognize the number.

"Hello," he said.

"Dominic, what the hell is going on? Why the hell you do Nu like that?"

Dominic still pissed off, went all the way in.

"Mannnn, don't nobody got time for NuNu childish ass and like I told her I'm tired of playing. She not about to keep leaving me with blue balls."

That statement got a laugh out of Mandy.

"Boy, why do y'all call it that?" She asked.

Dominic didn't find the situation funny.

"Cause that's what happens, what you mean?"

Mandy laughed again.

"If you don't take a cold shower and get over it. Y'all boys be losing y'all mind if y'all can't hit like it's the end of the world," she said, while shaking her head against the phone.

That pulled a laugh out of Dominic because she was right, boys did act like it's the end of the world when it comes to not getting pussy.

"I mean, damn though Mandy why she be playing? She acts so hard but so soft at the same time. I thought she was ready because of how she was acting," he said.

"Nah, NuNu takes pride in her body, she puts on the front but she not ready."

"Man, she shouldn't be playing then, like for real a nigga don't have time for it." he shot back.

"Well maybe you should find a girl that's about that life just like you," Mandy said.

The way she said it made Dominic's dick jump. He knew when a girl was flirting, and Mandy was doing just that. She had always wanted Dominic, but he had wanted NuNu. Mandy had been jealous and envied NuNu.

When Mandy let those words slip from her mouth and he grew silent she knew then that he picked up on the meaning behind her words. She broke the silence. "Listen, I just called to tell you that you had her crying and that's not cool," and then hung up.

"Mandy why the fuck did you just say that," she said to herself. The phone rang and her heart raced. She knew it was him and she picked the phone up and saying hello.

"Can I come over and talk?" Dominic asked.

31

She was shaking her head no, but her mouth said yeah. Dominic hung up and Mandy prepared for his arrival. She was battling a lot of feelings within herself. NuNu was her friend and had been since the 9th grade. But since Dominic and NuNu had started dating she started having ill feelings toward her. She secretly always wished they would break up because she really wanted him for herself.

15 minutes later, Dominic was at her door and she took him in. He was short, with dark colored skin and with braids straight to the back. Mandy let him in locking the door behind her. She walked down the long hallway of the one-story home and called back "If you want to talk you better follow me and not just stand there." That's all Dominic needed to hear, and he was right behind her within seconds following her down the hall which seemed like it was leading to bedrooms, they entered and immediately started kissing. How Dominic knew this is what Mandy had wanted all along blew her wig back. They made their way to the bed and that was all she wrote.

Mandy snapped out of her thoughts, stood from the step and went into the house leaving Dominic standing there looking at her confused. He grabbed up his pen and notepad and followed right behind her. Locking the door behind him he shouted for her.

"Mandy, what's wrong baby?" He asked.

"You can stop with the shouting Nic, I'm sitting right here," she said.

He noticed her sitting in the recliner with her head hung low in her lap. He crossed the room and pulled her up from the chair, forcing her to take a seat on his lap.

"Talk to me baby, what's wrong?"

Mandy looked at him with teary eyes and a heavy heart. How she had let this happened, she couldn't understand. She was in love with a boy that should have been off limits. Mandy was breaking girl code and she couldn't help it. She had always been attracted to Dominic and she wanted what she wanted. And she wanted him. In fact, she needed him and had crossed a friend just to have him.

"Nic, this is wrong on so many levels and you know it. I can't continue to be around her knowing I have fallen in love with you, I just can't, and I won't. So, either we tell her together or I end this with you."

That last statement caught him off guard.

"Say what?" he asked.

Mandy just sat there, staring. He heard her, and she wasn't up for having to repeat herself.

"So, you mean to tell me you're willing to choose her over me?" Dominic quizzed.

"Yes, I'm going to choose my friend over you unless we tell her together. If I'm going to ruin a friendship you at least have to be worth it and stand by my side when it goes down Nic," Mandy said.

"Man, I don't see why you feel like you obligated to tell her anything Man Man," calling her by the nickname he gave her a few weeks after they had started messing around, "we were together 5 months," he stated.

"Nic I don't care if it was a week, I just can't keep this in no more and even though I know she is going to whoop my ass because of this, you have to be there to come clean with me," she said cutting him off.

33

Mandy lowered her eyes to her lap and Dominic tilted her chin up slightly forcing her to look at him. He loved Mandy, how it the feelings had crept up on him, he didn't know. However, now that it had he both hated and loved it at the same time. At first, it was just to make NuNu mad but as time passed, he started feeling Mandy and made her his girl. They had been rocking for the last 8 months and he wasn't willing to let her go. So, for her, he was going to do what she asked because he wasn't willing to lose her and with the ultimatum being set, he knew he had no choice but to agree to what she wanted.

"Okay Man Man, we can tell her together but if y'all get to fighting you better try to beat her ass, I can't have my girl out here getting dawg walked and shit," he said laughing and kissing her face. Mandy laughed slightly and kissed him back. Even though she was glad he agreed to her request she still felt fucked up about how things were going to go down, she knew that she wasn't only about to lose 1 friend but 2 because she knew Leah was riding with NuNu. She let out a sigh as she thought to herself, *only time will tell.*

CHAPTER FOUR

☐

*L*eah entered her god mother's house both hands filled with bags, after coming from the mall with NuNu. Leah's father had gifted her with five hundred dollars to spend on summer clothes, so she wanted to step her game up and shop at the mall instead of one of the hood stores. They had been shopping and talking for hours in and out of different stores trying on different items until they found what suited them and catching up on the latest news with the boys that had entered their life.

It was a party being thrown at Mandy's house for the end of the school year and the girls were coming to impress. NuNu knew Tyson would be there and Leah had every intention of inviting Marcus. She hadn't seen him since their walk in the park, but they talked on the phone when he wasn't busy making money. Every night for the past week and a half they talked and fell asleep on the phone with each other.

Leah called out for her god mom once she had gotten all her bags in her bedroom. She had moved in with her when she turned 11 and for the past 7 years, Stacy was just like one of Leah's best friends. She went to her about everything and never held one thing back from her god mommy. The way Stacy loved Leah you would have thought she had birthed her. Stacy and Leah's mom had been friends since Leah was

6 years old. Stacy had loved her since and automatically started calling Leah her daughter. She didn't raise children of her own however, her maternal instincts were always present when it came to Leah.

"Stephanie," Leah called out, calling Stacy by her real name playfully.

Stacy walked in Leah's room after a minute with her hand on her hip giving Leah a look that made her bust out laughing. Her godmother was the prettiest tomboy Leah had ever seen. Stacy wore Nike basketball shorts and a Nike t-shirt. She was half white and half black, with short blonde and sandy brown hair.

"Hi g mommy," she said, turning on her little girl voice because she knew Stacy didn't play.

"Naw, don't try to be all sweet now when you just called me Stephanie like I'm the child and you the mama."

Leah laughed and walked across the room with her lip poked out and arms opened wide for her to hug Stacy. The two ladies embraced and then took a seat on Leah's bed. "So, mommy I met this boy," Leah said dramatically as she got comfortable laying across the bed with her arm resting over her forehead. Stacy turned her body, one leg folded on the bed and the other still hanging from it.

"Aww sucky-sucky now," Stacy replied with a smile. Leah had never been the one to talk about boys the way she started off the conversation about Marcus. She talked to them as friends but not in any other way. Leah blushed.

"Yeah g mommy, he dope, everything about him is hot."

"Well get to talking baby girl because I want all the details, he must be special if you are bringing him up to me."

"He is special, he's a little taller than me, dark skinned with full lips, oh those lips," Leah said with a small smirk.

Stacy rolled her eyes at Leah with all the dramatics. Leah noticed her rolling her eyes and paused smiling.

"What?" She asked.

"Nothing girl, finish telling the damn story," Stacy said.

Leah was talking about this boy as if he were the King of Toledo.

"We went for a walk in the park the first day we met and talked as if we had known each other for years," she sighed.

I know this girl bet not had fucked him already, Stacy thought to herself as she listened.

"We talk all day, every day when he's not busy working," Leah said, finally finishing her story.

"He has a job?" Stacy asked shocked.

Leah paused. She didn't want to tell her god mom that Marcus was a hustler. Stacy had always taught her that a dope boy was just a boy waiting in line to have prison numbers slapped on his back and work for the state making twenty dollars a month. So, Leah knew better. But yet she craved him. His presence always excited her. Leah didn't want to lie to her godmother, but she couldn't tell her that her teachings went in one ear and out the other when it came to this one boy. Omitted. Leah omitted by simply nodding her head and not specifying that Marcus chased illegal money. She hoped and prayed that Stacy didn't push for more information on her young love.

Stacy caught the pause. However, Leah was 18 years old and it was time to let her bump her head. Her god mom sensed all things when it came to her goddaughter, so she

37

knew Leah was holding something back. Stacy was a firm believer in everything coming to the light. In due time it would come out about what Marcus was involved in, so Stacy changed the subject.

"So, I guess that's who's been keeping you up all night, I come in here hearing both of y'all snoring on the phone," Stacy said while laughing at her god daughter's crushing phase.

"I do not be snoring," she hollered in laughter.

"Girl, like hell you don't. I heard both of y'all a few times."

"Well I want to invite him to Mandy's party and I'm kind of nervous since I haven't seen him in like a week."

"Daughter just call the boy and invite him. I'm not raising no scary woman so do what you want without regret just make sure you're doing what's right so that way later down the line you won't be singing your should of, could of, would of's at the end." Stacy paused for a moment and then continued, "I trust you to make the right decision about what to do and what not to do. You've been doing an amazing job Leah and I'm proud of you no matter what."

Leah smiled and hugged Stacy again before she pulled her phone out to call Marcus. Before she hit the talk button, she looked at her god mom and smiled while in the same notion asked for privacy so she could make the call. Stacy smiled while rolling her eyes, standing to exit the bedroom. Before she closed the door, she peeked her head back in the room, asking if Mandy's mother knew about the party. Stacy knew Mandy's mama was barely home and hardly ever paid attention to the child she had birthed. Leah nodded her head yes in response.

"I know you're probably thinking that it won't be any adult supervision there since her mama is never home but her auntie will be there watching g mommy."

Stacy smiled. Though Leah was grown.

"Yeah, that's exactly what I was thinking, the girl mama is never around and I'm surprised the fast tailed heffa hasn't turned up pregnant by now."

Leah laughed and just shook her head, she knew her god mom didn't play nor did she bite her tongue.

"Oh, and don't nobody want to hear your scary ass on the phone anyway," she said while shutting the door.

Leah smiled and then hit the talk button. She was hoping he would agree to the party because she desperately wanted to see him tonight.

"What's cracking?" Marcus said answering the phone.

Leah giggled at the way he answered his phone and responded with a *what's cracking?* of her own. Marcus laughed.

"Man, you want to be like me so bad don't you boo?" Leah beamed at the remark, just him calling her boo had sent flutters to her stomach.

"No, I'm not trying to be like you, but I am trying to be with you," she replied as she started biting on a nail.

Marcus's eyes grew wide and he stopped counting his earnings that he had just collected from his homie City. The statement caught him off guard. He smiled, licked his lips and thought about how to respond to her comment. Leah continued with the nature of the call after he didn't respond right away,

"So, my friend Mandy is having a party tonight and I'd really like for you to come if you're free," she replied as she started biting her nails again.

"I really don't do house parties boo, but you can send me the address and I'll come to swoop you when you're ready to bounce," he said as he whispered to his boy City to count up the money that sat at his feet in a duffle bag.

"Okay homeskillet, I will send you the address and hopefully you change your mind and at least come give me one dance," Leah said laughing slightly.

She removed the phone from between her and shoulder as she started to hit the end button. "Aye Leah!" Marcus called out to her. She looked down at the phone bringing it back to her ear.

"Yeah," she replied.

Marcus blew out a sharp breath. He was about to say something that he wasn't to certain of but he felt the need to just say it.

"About you wanting me," he said, releasing another sharp breath. Leah's heart dropped, she wasn't expecting him to reply to her statement from earlier, she held her breath in anticipation.

"Well, I want you too. I've never done the serious girlfriend thing, but I want it with you."

Leah finally exhaled and smiled. She couldn't hide the excitement as she let out a light scream. Marcus laughed, "chillax boo, we will talk more when I slide through to get you later, and I just might break you down as well," he stated before hanging up. Leah's smile was wider than the Ohio River, as she laid back across her bed she couldn't help but feel ecstatic about what the night would bring.

Leah hopped on the phone with NuNu and the girls started getting the night's details and began to plan what time they would be linking up to roll out to Mandy's house for the party. Leah had a few things to do around the house before she could actually start to get ready for the evening festivities. She walked into the living room and saw her god mom was laying across the couch reading a novel by Omar Tyree called *Flyy Girl*.

"G mommy, what all did you want me to do again?" Leah asked as she stood in front of Stacy.

Stacy laid the book on her chest.

"Nothing baby girl, just start doing what you need to do for the party and I'll handle the small chores around the house I got you covered."

"Now that's wassup," Leah said as she leaned down and kissed her god mom on the cheek. "Thank you," she squealed before heading back to her room to start getting ready.

The party started at 10pm and Leah checked her phone seeing that she had two and a half hours to get ready. She showered and dressed putting on blue Baby Phat jean shorts with an orange Baby Phat shirt and orange sandals to match. She wore her hair down bumping the ends and adding big gold hoop earrings. She slid her gold *L* ring back on her finger and applied her 16-inch gold rope chain that held and *L* on it as well. She looked in the mirror and was impressed with her appearance.

Leah headed toward the front room when she heard NuNu talking with Stacy.

"When did you get her Nu?" She asked.

NuNu looked at her friend.

"Okay then miss thing, now that's hot." NuNu piped.

Leah gave her friend a wink.

"Let's bounce."

The girls headed for the door and Leah turned back around and said, "love you, g mommy. I'll see you later." Stacy returned the sentiment and told the girls to have fun and be safe.

"Call me if you need me, daughter," she also said.

"I will," Leah replied, shutting the door heading to Mandy's.

CHAPTER FIVE

☐

*T*here were so many people swarming throughout Mandy's house as Leah and NuNu entered the spot. 702's *Where My Girls* oozed through the huge house speakers as Mandy's older cousin Justin who was the DJ, was putting together tracks to keep in rotation. Leah led NuNu through the crowd of people, one arm in the air as they found a spot to dance.

Where my girls at
Well is you feelin that
Put one hand up
Can you repeat that

The two girls snapped their fingers, pointing from the front to back and danced to the beat as they laughed. Mandy spotted the duo and joined them matching the vibe. Mandy took in Leah's appearance and loved what she saw.

"Leah boo that's hot!" She said complimenting her.

"Thanks, *biotch*!" Leah said laughing.

NuNu smiled at her two friends but that smile instantly faded once she spotted Dominic across the room.

"Mandy, what the hell is he doing here?" NuNu asked with a look of disgust on her face. "Nu, be nice, he here with some of the other boys," Mandy said telling half of the truth.

He was really there for her, but she couldn't just come out and say that, it wasn't the right time. If NuNu was mad at his presence alone she would for sure be blazing at the secret that Mandy was holding in.

"Nu, don't pay him any attention, we're here to kick it not let that busted nigga make you upset, matter of fact, Tyson big head ass just walked in the door," Leah announced as she pointed. NuNu spun on her heels so fast at the mention of his name and immediately rushed to him.

A crispy black t-shirt draped off his basketball player's frame. He wore black and red Girbauds, and a pair of matching Air Force Ones graced his feet. This boy was so fucking fine and NuNu wanted to devour him. She was amazed that she was able to keep some restraint the night they were at his house. However, tonight all her self-discipline was withering away. She completely forgot about Dominic killing her vibe when Tyson entered the party and she was happy that he showed up. Mandy looked to Leah with eyes of shock.

"Her ass is head over hills for that nigga, you see how she just bounced on us once you said he was here?"

"I see but forget all that, let's dance," Leah said as she grabbed Mandy by the arm and started dancing to Mystikal's *Shake Ya Ass* that was now currently playing.

Shake ya ass, but watch ya self
Shake ya ass, show me what you workin with

44

Shake ya ass, but watch ya self
Shake ya ass

Leah had her hands on her knees poppin so hard that it looked like she'd break her back and Mandy encouraged her every step of the way. Then the girls switched places, it was Mandy's turn to show out and she did just that. Dominic was watching her from across the room as the girls drew attention to themselves while dancing. Mandy caught a glimpse of Dominic and started showing off even more. She was putting on a show for him and she knew that he loved the sight of her small frame and nice size booty shaking for him and only him. She smiled once he gave her a wink but instantly grew nervous, hoping that no one caught the gesture. She knew that they would have to tell NuNu soon because now it was starting to get more serious and she was tired of hiding and acting as if what they had was only for them to know. She was ready to let the world know that she loved him, and he loved her. Leah noticed the disturbed look on Mandy's face and stopped dancing asking her friend what was wrong.

"Nothing, I need to get something to drink that's all, will you come with me to the kitchen?" She asked. Leah nodded and followed Mandy to the kitchen taking a seat on the bar stool that was in front of the kitchen island. She leaned her arms on the island and then had to do a double take because she knew she didn't just see a roach crawling across the damn counter. *That's nasty,* she thought to herself. Leah moved her arms from off the counter and sat there no longer wanting anything to drink if it wasn't coming from a can or bottle.

45

Mandy walked over to Leah with two cans of Pepsi handing her one and then opening hers.

"So, you want to tell me your sudden mood change, Amanda?" Leah asked.

Mandy knew when Leah called her that she was serious and wasn't with the *oh nothing is wrong act*. Mandy sighed.

"I have a lot going on Leah and I have no one to talk to."

"You have me, Mandy, what are you talking about?" Leah interrupted her.

"That's just it, Leah it's certain things I don't know how to tell you or even begin to explain to you," Mandy said.

"Girl we're friends you can tell me anything no matter what it is that's what me and Nu are here for, we're your girls so talk to us no matter what, okay?" Leah stated firmly.

"Okay," Mandy replied, still feeling messed up because only if Leah knew what storm was getting ready to come, she would be singing a different tune right now.

"Let's get back to the party," Mandy said, taking a sip of Pepsi.

Leah sat her can down on the island not even wanting it no more after seeing the roach. The girls entered the living room noticing that people were making their way down to the basement. Mandy led Leah down the basement steps, following the crowd. There were red lights illuminating throughout the basement and the atmosphere was perfect. Huge speakers were lined up across the wall and the music was still bumping even though the DJ was upstairs. Leah spotted NuNu and Tyson off in the corner of the basement talking. Tyson had his arms around NuNu, and a bright smile was on her face. Leah loved the sight. NuNu had wanted

Tyson for the longest and finally got her man. As Leah and Mandy made their way through the basement, people were gathered everywhere. It was safe to say that Mandy's party had turned out to be a success. Leah was taken a back when she saw Marcus come through the crowd of people looking smooth as ever. He wore light blue Sean John jeans and a white and blue Sean John button down shirt. She headed straight toward him and wrapped him in a hug so tight Marcus thought she would cut his oxygen off.

"I see some dime is happy to see me," he said with a smirk.

"I am, I didn't think you'd come being that this is not your scene," she replied with a wide grin.

"Well, I told you I just may show up to give you a dance and I felt in the mood to break you off," he said with the most beautiful smile that made Leah kitty start to purr.

As if Justin knew what Leah's music selection would be for the perfect first dance, she heard *Hey Mr. DJ* croon through the speakers.

"Oh my god Justin is the shit for playing this," she said snapping her fingers.

She looked at Marcus.

"You and me now since you think you can break me off, let's see what you got."

"Lead the way," Marcus said, licking them full chocolate lips that always made Leah weak.

"Oh, you ain't said nothing but a word," Leah replied.

She took Marcus by the hand and backpedaled to the middle of the floor where there was space and spun around with her back pressed up against his front. With one arm still

47

in the air she started slowly moving left to right with the beat grinding against him.

Let the music play
Cause I want to get it on
Put your arms around me, baby, oh yeah
And let's start a slow grind, grind
I'm gonna rock and roll, rock it all night

Leah was breaking Marcus off as she winded her hips and dipped low so seductively. However, Marcus was far from an amateur as he matched her vibe and dipped as well, grinding against her. His moves impressed the hell out of her as he swayed left to right crossing his arms in an X while she bent over grinding her ass right back against him. If people didn't know any better, they would have thought they were fucking the way he was hitting it from the back. All eyes were on them.

You're the only one I want to slow dance with
DJ let the record spin around real nice and slow yeah
You're the only one I want to slow dance with
All you gotta do is take my hand

NuNu was gassing her friend up in excitement. "Leah, you better break his ass down," she yelled.

Leah laughed and continued to work her boo as he did the same. The song ended and the pair hugged. Leah was all smiles. She tried to break their embrace, but he stopped her.

"Don't move just yet baby, my boy hard," Marcus whispered.

Leah laughed hard at his comment, she knew then that she had done her thing with that dance.

"Mission accomplished," she whispered back to him.

He laughed and adjusted himself while she still stood in front of him. Once he was done, he and Leah started to move to a secluded part of the basement until she heard NuNu get loud. She snapped her neck in the direction of the commotion and headed to her.

"Bitch, how the fuck could you cross me like this? NuNu shouted at Mandy.

Mandy looked at Leah as she was approaching with tears in her eyes. She knew the situation was about to get ugly. *I just had to fuck with this nigga,* she thought. "Tell her you scandalous bitch, tell her what the fuck you and this bum ass nigga been doing behind my fucking back. TELL HER!" NuNu screamed again.

"What in the world is going on? Nu stop yelling," Leah said calmly.

Since Mandy wasn't talking fast enough for NuNu, she bit into her bottom lip and punched Mandy straight in the mouth. Mandy hit the floor and all hell broke loose.

"This bitch been fucking Dominic," NuNu yelled as she attacked her friend again.

She was a loose cannon and couldn't be stopped, she was landing blows all over Mandy's face. Mandy tried to fight back and that only made matters worse for her, NuNu started dawg walking her ass, she began dragging her all over the basement. Dominic tried to get NuNu off Mandy but that was definitely the wrong move with Tyson standing there. Tyson slid out his shirt and pounced on Dominic's short ass, stomping him straight out. He had never liked the young nigga from the story NuNu told him and him placing hands on her, gave him every right to whoop his ass behind his lady.

Leah couldn't believe what she was seeing or what she had just heard. She grabbed NuNu and pried her off Mandy and had Marcus do the same with Tyson and Dominic. The entire night just spiraled out of control and someone had to get it together. Justin flew down the stairs to assist with the chaos as well as Mandy's aunt.

"You dirty bitch," NuNu yelled out once more while still trying to attack Mandy.

Mandy was crying so hard she was hyperventilating. She tried to get out the words I'm sorry, but it came out jumbled as her chest heaved up and down.

"Fuck you, the I'm sorry and that nigga, you weren't sorry when you were laying on your back with the very nigga that played me. Naw, keep that shit. Leah please get off me I just want to get the fuck out of here," NuNu yelled, pushing Leah off her. Marcus was able to get Tyson to chill down, telling him to go calm his girl. Tyson slid his shirt back on and started walking away, yelling back behind him at Dominic, "this ain't over dawg!"

CHAPTER SIX

☐

*M*arcus and Leah sat in the car outside of his house in silence after leaving Mandy's party. Leah had so many things going through her head about the events that had just taken place.

"How can boys be such dogs?" she asked, finally breaking the silence.

Marcus gave her a confused look. "No, what you should be wondering is why your homegirl would do some foul shit like that to her friend?" Marcus shook his head as he continued, "That was some messed up shit on both of their ends but more so hers because she has been down with y'all since 9th grade, right?"

"Yeah you're right baby she has and I can't believe she would be so scandalous. Marcus, I can't lie it took everything in me not to molly wop her ass right along with Nu." Leah replied. He looked at her shocked. He had never met girls that stuck together, the way Leah and NuNu did. He knew then that their bond was something different and he respected it.

"You wanted to jump in?"

"Yeah, I did, I have known Nu since the 5th grade, that's my sister and she will always come first and the shit Mandy

51

and Nic pulled was some straight ho shit. Matter of fact take me back to-"

Marcus didn't even let her get the rest of her sentence out. He silenced her with a kiss, sticking his tongue in her mouth. Leah was taking off guard but submitted melting into him as their tongues danced. She needed this distraction, wanted it desperately in fact. Marcus had her in a mood while they were dancing because he was matching her vibe and the way he hit her ass to each beat had her panties soaking. Now here his chocolate ass was kissing her, igniting the flame in between her legs all over again.

"Marcus... Baby..." Leah whispered in between rotating her head from left to right while he stole her tongue. *Damn this nigga can kiss.*

"Yeah, bey," he replied, never breaking the rhythm.

"We have to stop or we are going to be sexing all over this car," Leah stated.

Marcus tilted her head slightly to the right and started running his tongue down her neck, stopping at her collarbone and then back up to her ear, nibbling ever so softly. Leah let out a low moan and started caressing his chest as he kept assassinating her earlobe. Marcus started reaching inside her shorts as he kept that tongue glued to her body traveling down her neck again. He finally got his hands inside her panties, and it was he who let out a moan followed by "damn bey, let's go in the house." Marcus groaned before adjusting his boy that was standing at attention.

"Where's your mom?" Leah asked in hesitation.

"She here but my room's in the basement and she won't hear you," he said, smiling in amusement.

52

He opened his door, hopping out and rushing around to the passenger side of the car to help Leah out. They walked hand and hand to the side door and down a flight of stairs that led to a fully finished basement. This section of the house looked like a small efficiency apartment. They came upon a room in the back of the basement which was Marcus's bedroom. Leah took a seat on the bed when they entered as she watched her boo lock the door and kick off his shoes. He moved toward the bed and kneeled in front of her as he stared at her, he felt something stirring in him. He never had this feeling before getting ready to smash a chick, but with Leah it was special. He lifted toward her slightly and began to kiss her. Leah stuck her tongue in his mouth getting aggressive and started unbuttoning his shirt. Marcus helped her and then stood before her revealing his lean body. He wasn't muscular but he wasn't boney either, to Leah he was perfect. She was ready to indulge in this piece of chocolate that was standing in front of her. She had just unwrapped her Mars candy bar and she knew that it was going to be worth the stomachache. She started to remove her clothing, but Marcus stopped her, "Let me do the honors bey." She bit her lip seductively as she watched him undress her until she was fully naked. He laid her down while kissing her neck and then made his way to her perfectly shaped *B* cup breast. Marcus grabbed the stereo remote from his nightstand and turned the radio on, all while still giving attention to Leah's erect nipples. Ironically R. Kelly *Sex me* began crooning throughout the room. *Yeah, this was definitely meant to happen,* Leah thought.

I feel so freaky tonight
And I need someone to make me feel alright
So, bring your body her baby
Lady have no fear
I'm going to fulfill your fantasy
Just as long as you….. Ooooohh… sex me

Marcus started playing with Leah's wetness as he continued to suck her breast. He paid the most attention to the right one noticing that it was her most sensitive side and made her juices rain down on his fingers even more. He slid out of his pants and boxers, climbing back on the bed with her. Leah was squirming in anticipation and couldn't take it any longer, she was so horny, and her womanhood ached.

"Marcus, baby come on put it in," she said.

In one smooth motion, he slid up in her with a low grunt. "Damn!"

He was taken aback at the way her pussy was gripping his boy. He knew Leah wasn't a virgin but what he didn't know was that she hadn't been tampered with in over two years. She was tight and wet, she should have given him a fair warning because in this moment he didn't stand a chance. Leah moaned as he rocked in and out of her slowly trying not to bust so quick. *Damn this shit really biting down on a nigga*, Marcus thought. Leah let the passion she was feeling flow in his ears, sending even more excitement through Marcus. He felt himself about to explode so he retreated from inside her and went downtown.

"Oh shit," Leah said as her eyes got wide from shock and pleasure.

Marcus was a freak. He was licking and sucking on her as if he had done this a time or two before. Leah had always heard that dark-skin boys were freakier when it came to sex but damn, she didn't think it would be this good. Marcus inserted one finger slowly as he licked her clit and then two noticing that her vagina gripped his fingers with a vice grip. *I can't let no one else hit this shit after me,* he thought as he continued to work his tongue and fingers. He was already trademarking her sex. He couldn't allow another nigga to sample his plate.

Sex me, baby, baby
Sex me, baby, baby
Sex me, baby, baby

Leah was grinding to the beat of the music on Marcus's tongue and fingers as she worked her way to an orgasm. "Ohhh my god," she cried out as she closed her legs around his head and shook from the vibration erupting through her body. Leah's whole body went numb from the tingling feeling, she snapped her eyes shut and put an arm across her face. Marcus climbed up her trailing kissing along the way until he met her lips and slid his boy right back in her since she had gotten her pleasure. He moved her arm from her face and played in her hair while pushing back and forth in her wet walls. Leah pushed him off her and made him lay on his back, she was about to take him for a ride he wouldn't forget. She climbed on top and started rocking slowly on him as he bit his balled fist from the pleasure. Once she leaned forward and started licking his ear, it was a wrap, it was nothing he could do with this girl. She started going up and down fast and then slow still keeping the beat of the music playing through the radio. Leah heard his toes cracking and once she felt him stiffen inside her she picked up her pace because she knew he was about to cum.

"Leah.. damn baby... I'm about to nut," he moaned.

She hopped up just in time and started stroking his manhood, which that only intensified his pleasure. Marcus bit into a bawled fist.

"Damn girl," Marcus called out and then a small chuckle followed after that.

"You're going to make a nigga want to marry you the way you just put that shit down, Damn."

Leah found humor in his statement as she climbed off the ride smiling and snuggled next to him.

*L*eah woke up the next morning to the smell of her god mom making breakfast. She had slept until eleven and was extra hungry. She made her way to the kitchen and stood in the doorway as she watched Stacy sing and dance to Mary J. Blige's song *Real Love*. Stacy turned around noticing her daughter watching her, "girl get in here and have a seat." Leah crossed the kitchen and took a seat at the table hoping and praying that her g mommy wasn't about to cut into her for coming home at 5 o'clock in the morning.

"Did you have fun last night?" Stacy asked as she added cheese to the eggs, she was making for them.

"Yeah it was okay until it ended up chaotic," Leah replied as she yawned, still exhausted from last night's chain of events. She smiled at the thought of Marcus and was snapped out of the thought when Stacy asked with concern about what was so chaotic.

"Mandy and Nu got into a fight mommy, and Nu dawg walked her throughout the whole basement."

"What in the hell you mean they fought?" Stacy asked as she cut the stove off and went to grab plates.

"Mandy been messing with Nu's ex-boyfriend behind her back and I guess Mandy felt the need to tell her last night, so it got crazy."

"Whatttt?" Stacy said. "That girl fast yes I know, but to be fucking her friend man behind her back is scandalous as hell, did you jump in and help my girl?" Stacy asked while handing Leah a plate of potatoes, eggs with cheese, sausage and buttermilk biscuits.

"G mommy, can you hand me the jelly please?" Leah pleaded as she dug into her plate of food.

"And no, I didn't but I wanted to," Leah said, finally answering the question. Stacy strolled over to the fridge as requested to seize the jelly before taking a seat at the table with her baby to eat breakfast and finish chatting about everything that had taken place last night.

"So, did your honey dip ever show up?" Stacy asked. Leah looked up from her plate and gave Stacy a smirk.

"Of course, he showed up for ya girl," Leah replied, taking a bite of her biscuit. Stacy hollered in laughter and shook her head at Leah's confidence.

"Okay now, don't think you all that just cause his ass came to see you and showed you a good time," she said.

The look on Leah's face at the mention of a good time had her feeling transparent like her god mom knew Marcus had indeed shown her a good time last night.

"You can stop looking like that girl," Stacy said, interrupting Leah's thought.

"I know what took place last night and we don't have to discuss it and like I told you before you left out of this house last night, make decisions you won't regret later." Silence fell over the kitchen for a brief second as Leah played back last night in her mind. *Nah I don't regret it at all*, she thought as she picked her fork back up, finishing her breakfast.

CHAPTER SEVEN

☐

*L*eah and NuNu sat on top of the picnic tables, watching the boys play basketball. Two weeks had passed since the catastrophe at Mandy's party and the girls hadn't spoken on it whatsoever. When Leah tried to bring it up, NuNu would cut her off simply telling her she didn't want to dwell on Mandy's trifling ass. Leah was watching Marcus shake some of the boys on the court and cheered him on every time he hit a 3-point shot. For every shot he made, she would keep track because that's how many times she planned to peck his full lips at the end of the game.

NuNu was in her thoughts and Leah could see it. "Nu are you ready to get this out of your system? It's been two weeks and you won't talk about it," she said as she turned to face her. NuNu shook her head not wanting to discuss the elephant in the room, she had written Mandy off and wanted round 2 just off GP. She told herself if she caught Mandy walking around, she would dust her ass one last time before just leaving the situation alone altogether. She was happy with Tyson, so it wasn't like she was fighting over Dominic, she wanted to whoop Mandy ass again for the disrespect and the betrayal. So, she swore once she caught her it was going down, no matter when or where and she meant that with everything in her.

"Nu! We are going to talk about this now." Leah said snapping her out of her thoughts. "Leah it's nothing to talk about honestly, me and that hoe can never be friends again, I'm not accepting any apologies at all."

"Has she tried calling you?" Leah asked.

"Yeah, she has been blowing me up and I just let the phone ring. She left a voicemail which I never listened to because like I keep telling everyone, I'm over it but when I catch her, I'm beating her ass and moving on from it. Leah if you choose to still be friends-"

"*Biotch,* don't play with me," Leah spat stopping NuNu from finishing the ridiculous sentence that was leaving her mouth.

She couldn't believe NuNu had fixed her mouth to let those words come out. They were sisters and she would always ride for her. Leah wanted to smack NuNu for even having the audacity. There was no way she could remain friends with Mandy after that shit. For all Leah knew she would probably try Marcus and then she would have to mop her ass over him.

"You're my sister and I wanted to jump in and beat her ass with you, but you had it, so I let you handle your business. Matter of fact I wanted Marcus to take me back over there because I wanted my round with her as well. I've known you since 5th grade and what she did I can't get with even if the act wasn't against me. So she no longer has a friend in me either, but I should have known something was up that night cause she was acting weird. Hell, she been acting weird for the last few months like the shit been eating away at her."

60

"Yeah well my fist going to eat away at her fucking face," NuNu said as she punched the air
with four quick punches.

Leah laughed so hard tears started falling.

"Girl, you a fucking trip," she said as she wiped her face.

"But anyways, what's been going on with you and Tyson bighead ass?" Leah asked, changing the subject.

"Girl stop talking about my baby head damn," NuNu said with a grin.

The thought of Tyson or even just hearing his name always made NuNu smile. She was completely head over hills for this boy and Leah could see it all over her face.

"Nu, you fell in love with him, haven't you?" she asked as she looked at her friend in awe. "I have Leah and I didn't even see it coming. I've always had the biggest crush on him but never in a million years would have thought we'd end up here." She stopped talking for a moment and shook her head. She couldn't believe that she finally found someone that was with her for her and didn't just want what was between her thighs. NuNu continued.

"I love that boy and I feel it in return from him, I mean really feel the genuine love from him."

NuNu had let this east coast boy with swag come along and sweep her off her feet. She had fallen hard for him and just hoped he wouldn't turn out to be fraudulent. Even at her age, NuNu saw forever with him and she prayed that the feeling was mutual. Leah was so happy for her friend, she wrapped NuNu in a hug telling her how thrilled she was for her and that she deserves all the happiness in the world.

"I know Tyson loves you as well," Leah stated.

"Why you say that?" NuNu giggled.

"Honey, listen if you could have seen how he was rocking Dominic stubby ass, you would have been proud."

NuNu threw her head back in laughter as they broke their embrace.

"How are things going with Marcus?" She inquired, still smiling ready to hear about her best friend's current situation.

"Well things with Marcus are going well, I mean really well," Leah said, taking a seat back on the table.

"I didn't know him and Tyson knew each other like that though," she added.

"Yeah, I didn't know either until the night after the party. Maybe we all can start getting together to do double dates."

"We will see, girl you know how those boys are, they be acting like they're too cool for all that," NuNu said, chuckling slightly.

NuNu just so happened to look across the street and raised an eyebrow.

"Well, well, well what do we have here," NuNu said as she stood up from the picnic table while sliding her rings off of both hands and sat them down.

"Girl, why are you taking off your shit like you about to scrap?" Leah asked as she started taking her jewelry off following suit, she didn't know what was about to go down, but she still knew to be ready for whatever. NuNu took off running across the court in between the boys, damn near knocking Marcus over.

"Damn, what the fuck," he yelled.

"Nu," Leah screamed as she took off running right behind her.

She spotted Mandy and knew then she was the reason they were in pursuit. "Marcus come on, she is about to scrape this girl again," she shouted back for him. NuNu had spotted Mandy walking from the corner store across the street from the basketball court and was about to get her last round in with the backstabber she once called a friend.

Everyone at the courts noticed the commotion and tailgated behind the girls. When Mandy caught wind of NuNu and Leah she dropped her bag of chips, Now and Laters and Faygo peach pop and took off running. "Shit," Mandy shouted as she ran as fast as she could. She forgot NuNu ran track and had speed with those short legs of hers. NuNu had caught Mandy and tackled her to the ground.

"Bitch!" NuNu shouted.

She smacked Mandy first, then wrapped one hand around her crimped ponytail cocking her fist back with the other and striking her over and over again. Mandy screamed while trying to block her face and bucking her body, trying to get her ex-friend off her. Leah caught up and didn't hold back.

"Bitch, what the fuck was you thinking huh?" She spat not letting up, raining punches on her.

Mandy tried everything she could to fight the girls off, kicking and swinging wildly to protect herself. She got a little relief once she heard Marcus's voice and felt him pulling Leah off of her. "Y'all chill the fuck out!" He barked. She still had NuNu to deal with and she knew she wouldn't be easy to handle. NuNu hit Mandy with a clean jab to her left eye, swelling it. She screamed in pain, seeing white from the blow.

"DAMN," everyone said almost in unison as they cringed from the sound. Mandy heard Tyson yelling for NuNu to stop while pulling her up.

"Nu'Asia, chill lor mama," he stated as he bear hugged her, trying to get her to calm down. "Ty get the fuck off me please," she shouted as she began to cry.

NuNu wasn't in the mood to be tamed. She was letting out anger from betrayal and frustration. She never thought one of her best friends would do the ultimate hurt. She had run to Mandy first when she and Dominic first broke up. It was Mandy's shoulder she cried on and for her to turn around and pull this hurt her beyond words could explain.

"Tyson let them fight one on one or it's just going to be worse cause NuNu is not going to stop," Leah told him as she was still being held back.

"Naw, fuck that my lady not about to be out her clowning," Tyson said as he picked NuNu up and carried her to his car that he left running after pulling up recklessly.

He wasn't with letting girls fight, he found it to be silly. They had already got a round in and NuNu had proven then she was with the smoke so there was no need to continue with the drama.

Mandy stood up with tears falling, one eye swollen and embarrassed as everyone stood around and watched the action.

"I'm so sorry Nu I swear I am. Please, I don't want to fight anymore," she pleaded.

"Bitch you should have thought about that before you went behind her back and was fucking her old nigga, *TRUE* friends don't do shit like that," Leah said as she advanced on Mandy.

"Leah... Get your ass back here," Marcus shouted, pulling her back in the opposite direction by the arm.

Tyson had NuNu pinned against the back of his car, whispering something in her ear. She nodded as she listened to what he was saying. He was always able to calm her down and she loved that about him. NuNu turned facing toward Mandy. "Bitch you've been touched by an angel," she said as she climbed in the car and leaned her seat back.

Leah turned heading towards Tyson's car but not before turning back and calling Mandy a scandalous ho. Everyone standing around started chanting, "Yoouuu's a hooeee!"

Mandy was filled with embarrassment as she jetted home, not stopping until she made it inside, locking the door behind her. She hadn't expected to be spotted by the girls or anyone else for that matter and was mad at herself from wanting that damn Faygo peach pop and watermelon Now and Laters so bad. She crossed the living room in hast, making her way to her bedroom where Dominic laid still sleeping.

"Nic get up please," she cried as she began coming out of her clothes. Dominic didn't budge which caused Mandy to yell with authority.

"DOMINIC GET UP NOW!"

She moved toward him and pulled the cover back. He laid there naked, dick hanging to the side with her dried juices all over it. He stirred slightly from the movement of the cover and then was up once she smacked him across the face.

65

"Damn Man you tripping," he said sitting up right in the bed, once he saw her swollen eye with blood dripping from her eye brow, he was up on two feet ready to fuck shit up. He went to touch her face and she winced.

"What the fuck happened?" he barked as he looked her over.

"NuNu and Leah jumped me on my way back here from the store, Nu did this to my face Nic, she did this because of you. I should have never got with you, this was wrong," she cried hysterically as she covered her face and fell to the floor.

Dominic found his boxers, putting them on with urgency and then sat next to her, consoling her as she cried while burying her face in the center of his chest. Dominic was fuming on the inside. Her cries made his blood boil. Dominic clenched his teeth together, as his jaw flexed, and his temple throbbed.

"Shhh," he said soothingly.

He stroked her head softly. He had allowed this to play out the way it did and he cursed himself on the inside.

"I'm so sorry ManMan. I swear to god I am. I never expected to fall for you baby, the night this all happened it was really on some get back shit with NuNu. I was going to smash you and then throw it in her face, but I fell for you baby and I'm sorry. I'll make this right, for you I have to make this right so no more static comes your way behind me loving you." Dominic spoke with so much remorse in his tone. He felt guilty for the part he played that led to her assault.

Mandy lifted her head at that remark. Her face was a mess and feeling ugly as ever, she sniffed, wiping her nose with the back of her hand.

"I love you too Nic."

He grabbed her face, staring at her, "did you at least pinch the bitch?" he asked playfully. Mandy punched him smack dab in the chest and smiled slightly even though she didn't find it funny. "Look, I'm going to run you some bath water and get you cleaned up so we can figure out how to fix this between you two," he said as he stood from the floor and pulled her up with him. He escorted her to the bathroom and plugged the tub with a sock since she didn't have a stopper. As he started the water, trying to get the temperature just right, he dropped his head at the sight of looking at her face. He felt terrible because he was the cause of all of this. He knew Mandy had liked him first, but he went after NuNu instead because she was prettier and not easy like her. Had he taken the time to acknowledge the attraction she had for him she wouldn't have betrayed her friend to be with him. Dominic stood and wrapped her in a hug.

"I'm so sorry baby, I really am." He offered once more as he pecked the tip of her nose.

"It's okay Nic," she whispered as she squeezed him tightly.

"Will you get the radio please, so I can listen to music while I'm in this tub and relax, my body is aching so bad," she said.

"Yeah, baby I got you, anything else you want me to do?" He asked as he headed toward the door to seize the radio for her.

67

"No, I'm straight." She said as she started peeling out of her ripped t-shirt.

After he made his exit, Mandy started taking off her under clothes and walked toward the bathroom mirror. The medicine cabinet that held the mirror was opened and when she shut it the image staring back at her instantly made her eyes water. NuNu had done a number on her face. Mandy always had insecurities about the way she looked and now her reflection looked worse in her eyes. Tears flowed down her face as a million thoughts ran rapidly through her mind.

"Dominic," she called out to him as she turned to stop the running water behind her.

"Yeah," he said, voice barely audible as he reentered the bathroom.

Mandy slid in the tub getting comfortable but wincing once her head touched the back of the wall.

"Can you go to the store and get me a Faygo, Peach pop and some-"

"watermelon Now and Laters," he said, finishing her sentence with a smirk.

Mandy smiled as she closed the only eye that she could voluntarily and asked could he plug the radio up and set it on the end of the tub next to the candles that sat there from their rendezvous the previous night. Dominic did as he was asked, kissed her on the forehead and then headed out to get the snacks she requested from the store.

Once Mandy heard the front door close, she climbed out of the tub and went to her bedroom trailing water behind her. She stood in front of her dresser again looking in the mirror hanging on her wall over the dresser and then pulled the bottom right drawer open, taking a box out from under a pile of her clothes. She placed the wrapped box on the bed and headed back to the bathroom to soak her body.

She took a seat turning on the radio to 95.7. The station played nothing but oldies music and that's the type of music she was in the mood for while she relaxed. Kelly Price, *A Friend of Mine* was in mid play and had Mandy feeling fucked up. What were the odds of this actually being her life right now? She shook her head as her eyes prickled while singing the words to the song. She felt the lyrics and felt like it was NuNu singing this about her. Sliding all the way in the water she submerged herself and then came back up after about 20 seconds. She leaned her head against the tiled wall and cried hard from her soul, her life was a mess and she was filled with so much pain and guilt. Mandy's eyes popped opened and she screamed before being punched in the head.

"Leah, what the fuck are you doing?" Mandy cried.

Leah didn't speak. She pulled her by the hair trying to take her out of the tub but couldn't get a tight grip on her wet hair. Mandy screamed for Dominic as she tried to defend herself, trying to get up but slipped back into the tub, accidentally kicking the radio, sending it crashing up against the wall and making it fall into the water as a result from the impact. Leah jumped back in fear as she realized what had just happened. The lights started flickering and Mandy's body started convulsing from the electricity going through her body. Mandy splashed water everywhere as her body flopped wildly out of the tub and started smoking, frying her within minutes.

69

Leah was terrified. She backpaddled into the hallway with her hands to her mouth and eyes wide in disbelief as she looked at Mandy's body lying on the bathroom floor. "What the fuck did I just do?" She said in a hushed tone as she looked around the hallway frantically. "Mandy," Leah called as she headed back into the bathroom. "Mandy, please get up." She cried. Little bolts were shooting through the water on the floor were Mandy laid. Leah looked toward the front door and darted for it. She couldn't stay, she couldn't take the blame for it. She grabbed the doorknob and looked back towards the bathroom as tears fell down her face. She shook her head, opened the door and made her exit.

*D*ominic returned to the house and noticed it was dark in the hallway when he was sure he had left the lights on. "Mandy," he called, making his way down the hallway. He placed the stuff she wanted from the store on the couch. He didn't hear the radio playing and the smell that invaded his nostrils made his stomach turn. It smelled like a mixture of burnt beef, hair, and charcoal. *What the fuck?* He said to himself, noticing the lights were out in the bathroom as well and the smell of fried hair becoming stronger. He opened the door. "AMANDA, NOOO!" He screamed. Dominic rushed inside and saw sparks coming from the outlet where the radio was once plugged in. He ran to her bedroom to get his phone, snatching it up with shaky hands. His eyes watered as he placed the call.

"911 what is your emergency?"

"Please help meeee, I need an ambulance to 0001 Tecumseh St. *now* please!"

"Sir what is the emergency?" The operator asked.

"My fucking girlfriend was in the tub... and... and... and just hurry the fuck up man, please."

Dominic threw the phone against the wall shattering it as he fell on the bed crushing the box Mandy had placed on the bed. "Man, what the fuck did you do?" He screamed out, grabbing his chest as he cried. He was crying so hard he could barely breathe and was literally sick to his stomach. "NOOOOO!" Was all he could get out. His vocabulary was gone and knowing that Mandy was gone as well made him want to be with her. Dominic felt the box against his back as he rolled back and forth from the devastation of finding his love laying on the bathroom floor lifeless. He lifted slightly, pulling the box from up under him. He looked at it confused because he knew it wasn't on the bed before he left for the store. He opened it taking out a note and pregnancy test. He saw the test results on the stick and yelled in agony snapping it in half.

"AHHHH, she's fucking pregnant man," he howled, as he stood from the bed pacing the floor until he heard the loud knocks coming from the front door. He didn't hear the sirens from the ambulance but knew it had to be them knocking. He

71

raced for the door swinging it open so fast that it sent the knob through the plaster of the wall.

"She's in the bathroom down the hall, water is everywhere and the fucking radio is in the tub" he barked growing more angry than hurt in the moment.

Dominic tried to head back into the bathroom with the emergency respondents, but they stopped him dead in his tracks. Dominic protested. It was no way he wasn't about to be by her side.

"Sir, you need to do as you're told, have a seat and let us do our job." Dominic spun on his heels looking the man in the eyes as tears fell. "That's my fucking life in there, I can't just sit." Dominic had never experienced heartbreak until this moment.

"Well, you have no choice young man, have a seat now," the officer said in a calm but demanding tone.

Dominic wasn't trying to hear anything. He stared the officer in the eyes, sneering. He needed to be right in the mix as they worked on Mandy. Dominic heard one of the responders. "We're losing her, we have to get her to the hospital now!" He said. The EMC came flying down the hallways and rushed out of the house, putting Mandy in the back of the ambulance.

Dominic couldn't think straight, he felt it in his soul she was gone. He didn't even bother to chase after them as they took her out. He knew he would never be able to come to her crib and lay up with her and talk about their life plans with one another. Mandy had poured out her soul to him within these walls, they talked about the things she endured as a child growing up. He too had opened up about his upbringing

72

as well. Dominic rounded the couch and took a seat on the edge of it, noticing the note from the box in his hand still, he opened it. A letter addressed to him and Mandy's mother, Tracy.

Dominic and Tracy,
I am so sorry for the pain I will cause. Dominic... Baby... I'm
pregnant and I am so sorry I will be robbing you of the
chance to be a father. I love you and I hope you can....

He couldn't even finish the letter, he folded it back up and tucked it in his pocket. Dominic dropped to his knees head to the floor, pounding his fist against the wood while cursing Mandy inside of his head for taking herself and his unborn baby away from him.

CHAPTER EIGHT

☐

One Month Later…

*L*eah and Marcus had been laid up in the basement of his mama's house for the past month, only leaving when they were going out to get food or to make runs to the inner city to chop it with his boys every once in a while. They couldn't get enough of each other. They watched lifetime movies, ate, and sexed all the time. That was their everyday routine after finding out about Mandy's death.

Leah was relieved that Mandy had left a suicide note. She knew no one would question what really happened. Neither her nor NuNu attended the small memorial, but they did send their condolences to the family, especially to Mandy's aunt. It seemed like she took it the hardest being that she was the one that helped take care of her because her sister was a rolling stone and was hardly around once Mandy hit her freshman year in high school.

Leah laid in bed staring at the ceiling lost in her thoughts of what happened that day at Mandy's. She hadn't told anyone, not even NuNu. She had run non-stop back home and locked herself in her room for the remainder of the day. Confused and not sure of what to think or what to do she crawled in bed and buried herself underneath the covers as she cried for hours. Leah closed her eyes and Mandy's face appeared behind her lids. She opened her eyes quickly and sat up in the bed frantically. "What the fuck?" she whispered as she put a hand to her chest. She closed her eyes again and shook her head, "Leah chill, you're tripping," she whispered to herself.

Marcus entered the bedroom from taking a shower and Leah appreciated the distraction. "Baby I think I'm going to my god mom house for the weekend," Leah stated as she sat up in bed watching him dry his chocolate body. He was a vision. A beautiful sight to see.

"No, you not," he said as if she asked him instead of telling him.

"Yeah I am baby, I've barely seen her all month and I miss her, besides school is about to start back up in the next few weeks and I need to start getting back into my school schedule." She began making her way to the edge of the bed, never taking her eyes off him.

"Yeah whatever," Marcus said, dismissing the conversation.

Leah stood up and crossed the room, removing the towel from his hands and started finishing the job for him. She dried him off, applied lotion to his body and picked out his attire for the day. She laid out an all black Nike sweat suit with all black Air Forces Ones. Marcus had gotten used to Leah catering to his every need. She could tell he was upset about her going back home.

"I know you're not feeling me going home Marcus, but you know school is about to start up, so what are you going to do then?" Leah asked.

"It's whatever Leah, I ain't tripping let's go. I got shit to do, I'm taking you home while I'm out handling business."

Leah looked at him in confusion.

"What?"

"Look, you heard me. Get dressed and let's go," he said with an attitude.

Leah didn't know where the attitude came from all of a sudden but she wasn't going to press the issue. She dressed and packed her things. She was ready to roll ten minutes later. The car ride to her house was a silent one and it ate away at her. Marcus was so into the music playing on the radio that he hadn't noticed Leah staring at him, she caught his attention when she turned the volume down on his radio.

"Man, what you doing? Haven't you heard the rule of never touching a nigga radio?" He asked as he tried to cut the radio back up. Leah rolled her eyes.

"Marcus, you've been acting slightly different the past two days what's up? Talk to me," Leah said as she turned in her seat to face him.

She knew it was a problem, the attitude and then him wanting to drop her off so early in the day said it all. Marcus kept his eyes fixed on the road as he maneuvered in and out of traffic.

"Listen, ain't nothing up. We good Leah, we have been cooped up in that room for at least a month and I'm just giving you what you asked for," he said dismissively.

"Yeah whatever," Leah said, rolling her eyes and then turning back around in her seat as she stared out the window. Something was up and she knew it. They were fine for the last month, couldn't get enough of each other and now today he was acting funny after she said she wanted to go home. They pulled up to Leah's house and she climbed out of his car, opened the back door to grab her things from the backseat, without a word and went straight into the house not even looking back.

Leah entered the house and heard moaning coming from the back room as she sat her things down by the front door. "I just know she is not in here getting hit in the middle of the day," Leah said to herself out loud while shaking her head. "G mommy you so nasty," Leah yelled as she left right back out the door. It was a nice day, so she decided to walk the few blocks over to NuNu's house hoping she was there. As she strolled down her block, she saw Dominic riding a bike down the street coming her way. When Dominic realized it was Leah, he hopped off the mountain bike and advanced on her. He had been waiting to see her or NuNu since the memorial, that he too opted not to attend. He just couldn't see a picture of his love sitting on an easel and her ashes in an urn.

"Did y'all have to fucking jump her bitch?" He barked as he yanked her by the arm and trapped her against the brick wall that used to be an old bridge on her street.

"Dominic if you don't get the fuck off me, I'm going to have my nigga rock yo ass," Leah spat while struggling to free herself from his tight hold.

"Why did y'all embarrass her like that?" He yelled as he broke down, tears falling from his face. He hadn't meant to get physical with Leah, seeing her caused him to snap without thinking.

"She was fucking pregnant, WITH MY BABY, she took her life and my babies because of this shit," he screamed while beating on his chest. Leah recoiled at the revelation.

"She was pre... pregnant Nic?" Leah asked as she chocked on her words. She held a hand to her mouth in shock. *Oh my god.*

Tears immediately started accumulating in her eyes and regret coursed through Leah's heart. *I'm a murderer,* she thought.

"Yeah, she was and now my babies are gone man, they're fucking gone," he shouted.

"Oh my god, Nic I had no idea," Leah said, wrapping him in a hug. She could no longer keep those tears at bay, they streamed down her face like water sliding down a glass window on a rainy day.

"I'm so sorry, had I known she was pregnant, I would have never touched her or even allowed Nu to touch her," she whispered while still embracing him.

"Y'all was wrong for how y'all did NuNu though Nic and you know it," Leah stated.

"I know," he said, pulling back from her and taking a step back. "I never meant for any of this to play out the way it did to be honest. I truly was going to smash Mandy and then throw it in NuNu face and not give a fuck how it unfolded afterwards, but she got to my heart." he said lowly as he touched the left side of his chest.

Dominic took a seat on the curb and Leah followed him feeling sorry. She never would have guessed that this rude, ruthless boy sitting next to her could feel. He treated girls like they were one hit wonders, played them one time and never spoke to them again. She had no doubt in her mind that he would have done NuNu the same, it explained why he was so mad that he couldn't take her most prized possession from her and went after Mandy. However, here he was in love with her deceased friend and mourning the loss of their child. The lives she felt responsible for taking. Leah started feeling queasy. She was literally sick to her stomach being in Dominic's presence knowing her involvement in Mandy's death.

"I didn't know she was pregnant either until that day I got back to the house and found her body in the tub. I went to the bedroom to call 911 and I noticed she left the pregnancy test and this letter to me and her mom," he said, pulling the letter out of his front pocket.

"You haven't read it?" Leah quizzed.

"No, well I mean I read a sentence or two, but I couldn't bring myself to read the whole thing."

Leah took the letter from him opening it slowly as she looked at him with sympathy, "I'll read it for you. I can tell that love was really there between you two," she said. Leah took a deep breath as her eyes scanned the letter and then proceeded.

Dear Dominic and Tracy,

I am so sorry for the pain I will cause. Dominic… Baby… I'm pregnant and I am sorry that I will be robbing you of the chance to be a father. I love you and I hope you can find it in your heart to forgive me one day. Please take care, move on, and be happy. I hope you find another love like the one we experienced but please don't forget the one we shared. Also, for me will you please apologize to NuNu for the mess we created and the hurt we caused her. For me Nic PLEASE... Please tell Leah I'm sorry she was one of my first real friends and I know I disappointed her after she found out what we did.

Tracy,

You caused me so much pain. I've always felt like a motherless child, you were never home, and you always put your boyfriend before me. I tried to tell you for years that Richard was touching me, and you never listened. You left me to believe that it was okay or that it was all my fault. Why didn't you listen? Why didn't you protect me? I know you heard my cries for help while you were in the other room. He violated me every chance he got and you let him. You were my mother, you created me but failed to protect your creation. I hated you for years. Hated you for the lack of love, the lack of guidance. Was I that bad as a child? What made you not want to listen or protect my innocence? Me no longer wanting to live is all your fault. If my own mother doesn't want me then who does? How could you not love me, what did I ever do to deserve the way you have treated me? I just wanted your love, why couldn't you give me that?

I Love you Dominic take care and I'll be with you always

80

As Leah finished reading the last line tears were streaming down her face. She never knew that Mandy was battling issues with her mother, she was always cheerful and didn't show any signs that she was feeling the things she wrote in the letter to Dominic and her mother. She looked to her left and saw Dominic with his head hanging low and fist balled together pressed to his forehead as he sniffed back his own tears. He was visibly hurt. His heart didn't beat the same now that Mandy and their child was gone. And Leah was being mad disrespectful being in his space right now.

"Nic I'm sorry you're going through this," Leah cried as she stood dusting off the back of her jeans and then pulled him into an embrace. She knew he needed the embrace because she did too. She would live with this secret about Mandy's death and regret for the rest of her life. Mandy was still a major part of her life. The girls had been friends since the 9th grade. The trio was no longer a trio, there were only two remaining.

As they stood there hugging Leah saw Marcus pull up swiftly. She jumped back scared that he would hit them from the way he pulled up on the curb so recklessly. Dominic instantly got in defense mode, ready for whatever because he knew if he saw what was going on, he would assume exactly what Marcus was assuming.

"Nigga why the fuck you all over my bitch?" Marcus asked as he came up out of his Ralph Lauren t-shirt and tossed it on the hood of his car. Leah's neck snapped in his direction. *I know the fuck he didn't*, she thought. Leah scoffed. She couldn't believe the disrespect that flowed from his mouth, but she moved quickly to stand in between the

81

two She held her hand to Marcus's chest and one hand was in front of Dominic as she tried to keep them from fighting. Marcus shoved her out the way and swung on Dominic. He was so short and didn't stand a chance against Marcus, but he didn't back down. Dominic blocked his first punch by ducking and then coming up hitting Marcus in the chin with an uppercut. The hit shocked Marcus and made him beast on Dominic. Leah caught her balance, so she didn't fall and attempted again to get her man off Dominic.

"Marcus! Baby… stop it," she pleaded as she pushed Dominic out the way and was finally able to get in between the two boys.

"Marcus he wasn't all over me!" She yelled.

"You know Mandy is gone, I was reading the fucking letter she left for him and her mom."

Leah was trying her best to explain what he had just seen. She didn't understand how he could just automatically assume that she would be all over Dominic as if he hadn't already been with both of her best friends. She was baffled that he would even try to play her like she would be just as scandalous as Mandy was.

"Why the fuck did I just catch you hugging this nigga? HUH tell me that shit, you just like these other bitches a straight bopping ass bitch," he spat with nothing but venom.

"Excuse me," Leah said as she cocked her head back in stun.

Marcus had never spoken to her in the way he was, she couldn't believe her ears.

"Nigga, I'm far from a fucking bopper and don't you *EVER* call me a bitch again," she said as she mushed him in the forehead with her pointer finger and then stormed off in the opposite direction. Marcus looked to his left to see that Dominic had hopped on his bike and took off.

"City, park my car real quick while I go get this fucking girl man."

"Aight," City shot back as he climbed from the passenger seat and headed to the driver side to do what was asked.

Marcus turned on his heels as he grabbed his shirt from the hood of the car to go after Leah.

eah arrived at NuNu's and started pounding on the door in haste.

"Nu, open the door!" Leah shouted as she grew slightly nervous. She didn't know where Marcus was, but she wanted to be in the safety of her friend's home.

Ms. Andrea swung the door open in alarm.

"Leah, what's wrong baby?" She asked as she motioned for her to come in the house.

Leah quickly stepped in the house and kicked her shoes off in relief. She went to give NuNu's mother an explanation but grew concerned when she saw Tyson on the couch hugging NuNu as she cried. The situation with Marcus was no longer a concern with Leah. She crossed the room swiftly to get to her friend, she didn't know why but seeing her cry had tears building in Leah's eyes as she wondered what was going on. Leah took a seat on the couch next to NuNu as she started rubbing her back while asking her what was wrong. Tyson spoke before NuNu could even get it out.

"We went half on a baby and she scared now," he said, smiling. He was the only one happy with the news. Tyson wasn't lying when he told NuNu that he could wait for her body. And she made him wait. After giving him the pink slip, they had created life. His life. One he would cherish forever because it came from her. He loved NuNu and was glad that she was pregnant. It was nothing that he wouldn't do for her and the fact that his baby was having his baby warmed his heart.

"Boy shut yo ass up, talking about half on a damn baby," Ms. Andrea stated with a grin. *This boy is really happy*, she thought to herself.

"Ms. Andrea you already know I was knocking it out, cause you had to tell us a few times to go somewhere else with all that noise your daughter was making," he said with a smirk.

"TYSON!" NuNu yelled in embarrassment.

"And that's exactly how you were yelling my name," he said, winking at her.

NuNu was slightly perturbed at how Tyson spoke so loosely around her mother. It was like he didn't think before he spoke to anyone, it was no filtering Tyson's mouth. Nonetheless, his lewd mouth had NuNu salacious. Leah's eyes grew wide as golf balls at Tyson's broadcasted news and her tears finally started to fall. She placed a hand on

NuNu's belly and started singing "I'm gonna be an auntie, I'm gonna be an auntie," over and over. Leah's non-signing ass had got a smile out of NuNu as she placed a hand on top of her friends and wiped her tears.

"Leah, I don't want to mess up my dreams, I don't want to drop out of school," NuNu said as tears started sliding back down her face. It was always both girl's fear, becoming a teen mom. She had dreams that she wanted to chase after high school. A baby on her hip would only slow her down. NuNu wanted to attend college for business management and real estate. It was her desire to be a business woman. *How am I going to do all this with a baby?* She thought. Leah and Tyson both said, "I got you and you got this," in unison.

All three of them looked at each other and burst into laughter. Ms. Andrea walked up on her daughter, forcing her to stand for an embrace.

"I'm going to be right here baby. I'll be here every step of the way to guide you in the right direction," her mother whispered in her ear as they rocked back and forth hugging.

NuNu sighed in relief. She needed those words. She needed to hear that she had support from all angles. It gave her courage that she would be able to take on motherhood with the help from her very own and still go after her dreams.

"Thanks, mommy," NuNu said, wiping her eyes as she laid eyes on Tyson.

"I Love You, Ty," she mouthed followed by a smile.

"I love you more baby girl," he mouthed back with a wink.

Their love was undeniable. It could always be felt no matter what. Since their first encounter at Tyson's home, their love story was being written. Seeing the two of them interact made Leah smile, she was happy for her friend. However, the news of NuNu being pregnant caused Leah to think of Mandy being pregnant and then dying. The thought started filling her with so much remorse. She pondered on how she would tell NuNu that Mandy was pregnant, but the thought was interrupted with a knock at the door.

Marcus walked in and Leah became irritated, she had forgotten he was outside. Tyson walked over and dapped Marcus up and told him the news about the baby. "That's what's up my boy congratulations," Marcus stated before he made his way to Leah. Leah remained seated on the couch as Marcus stood in front of her, her arms folded, and lips poked out. He then grabbed her arms unfolding them as he pulled her up and whispered for her to come talk to him.

"No, I'm not talking to you," she whispered back as she moved from in front of him and started talking to NuNu.

Marcus shook his head. He didn't have time to play with Leah, and he wasn't about to cause a scene in someone else's home. Marcus walked over to Tyson dapping him up again and telling everyone he'd see them later. "No, the fuck you won't," Leah mumbled under her breath as he closed the door behind him.

NuNu heard her and had also noticed Leah's attitude toward Marcus.

"What was that all about?" she asked.

"Nothing boo, me and him into it and I just don't want to deal with him right now," Leah said only telling half the truth. She didn't feel like it was the right time to tell NuNu the whole story, she didn't want to upset her in any way and wanted the moment to stay about her and the news that she and Tyson just revealed.

Ms. Andrea had made her way to the kitchen leaving the teenagers in the living room talking. About 45 minutes later she called from the kitchen for everyone to come and eat. She had whipped up soft tacos for dinner.

"Nu I made your plate baby, I need to make sure you feed my grandbaby," she said smiling as she set the plate in front of her daughter.

NuNu rolled her eyes.

"Mom please don't start with all that, Please," she replied. *I know she is about to get on my nerves*, NuNu thought.

Tyson saw the irritable look on NuNu's face and laughed.

"Yeah, make sure you feed my baby like Ms. Andrea said."

NuNu rolled her eyes at him as well and smiled.

"Oh, he gets a smile with the eye rolling and I get a smart mouth," her mom said, smirking.

"And boy, you don't have to keep calling me Ms. Andrea, being that you and my daughter went half on a baby as you would say."

The whole room broke out into laughter.

"Okay Dukes, you got it," Tyson said as he finally took a seat next to NuNu and pecked her on the cheek before he began to eat with the ladies.

"Leah, what was wrong baby? Why were you knocking at the door like that earlier?" Ms. Andrea asked after remembering Leah had not answered her question from earlier.

Leah froze as she tried to come up with a quick lie. She didn't want to cause an uproar over the small dispute her and Marcus had. She thought it would be best not to spoil the moment, so she decided to keep it to herself. Leah said the first thing that came to mind. "Oh, I was being chased by a dog and was scared." Leah felt like she was betraying her friend with holding onto not one but two secrets. Her and NuNu had always told each other everything, down to the most irrelevant things. But there was no way Leah would ever reveal her darkest secret. They all sat around the table eating and talking about how school was about to start in the next few weeks. Leah hardly participated in the discussion. She was thinking about Marcus. She stayed another hour before she called it a night and walked home. Tyson had offered to drive her home. He didn't believe in letting women walk anywhere. Leah declined his offer, insisting that she needed the time alone to clear her mind and think things over.

Walking in the house, she saw her god mom laid out on the couch as the T.V watched her. Leah bent down and pecked her on the forehead before she made her way to her bedroom and laid across the bed. She was in deep thought. Her thoughts were heavy, mainly on her friends and all the news she had heard that day, she was exhausted and before she knew it, she had drifted off into a deep sleep.

CHAPTER NINE

☐

*L*eah groaned as she started to wake up the next day, she had slobber all over her mouth and face sticking to the pillow. That sleep was much needed. She was so tired that she still had on all her clothes. Leah never slept in regular clothes. She wiped her mouth and swept her messy her out of her face, as she began to stretch.

"Well look who finally decided to wake up," Marcus said as he sat on the chest that sat in front of Leah's bed.

"What the fuck yo stalking ass doing in my room," Leah shouted as she sat up in alarm. Marcus laughed as he stood and made his way around the bed to sit down next to her.

"You might want to wipe the rest of that damn slobber off ya cheek before you get to talking shit with yo ugly morning face," he said with a grin.

Leah was vexed by his comment, wiping at her mouth, then cheek as she rolled her eyes and stood to make her way to the bathroom to get herself together. Marcus pulled her back sitting her in his lap as he swept her hair out of her face. "I'm sorry bey," he said as he tried to kiss her lips, but before he could Leah blew her stank breath all in his face and laughed as he recoiled. "Damn, a nigga didn't want to enter the fucking dragon," he said as he laughed. "Go brush them choppers with yo nasty ass blowing that hot shit all in my face."

Marcus lifted her from his lap and tapped her on the ass playfully. Leah swatted at his hands and headed to the bathroom, brushed her teeth and washed her face before returning to her bedroom. She walked back into her room and saw Marcus hurriedly putting his phone in his pants pocket. She dismissed the behavior thinking nothing of it.

"Where's my god mom?" she asked, taking a seat on the chest this time instead of the bed.

"She let me in like an hour ago and said she was going up to Detroit to the MGM Grand Casino to gamble and eat."

"Oh," Leah said simply as she crossed her arms and grew silent.

Leah really had no other words for Marcus at the moment. She was still pissed about his actions from yesterday and didn't want to be bothered with him today. If she was being honest with herself, she didn't want to be bothered with him ever again. Marcus shoving and calling her a bitch had left a bad taste in Leah's mouth. She had never endured disrespect from any boy, and she wasn't about to start with this one.

"Why you sitting way over there?" Marcus asked as he patted the space next to him, motioning for her to come sit next to him.

"Naw, I'm good, but you can tell me why your stalking ass has been here a whole hour watching me sleep?" Leah said as she remained planted in her seat. *That's some weird shit.*

Marcus ignored her question as he stood up rounding the bed and sat on her lap.

90

"Get your heavy ass off me boy, damn," Leah said as she struggled to push him off of her.

Marcus started licking her ear while she fought against him. He knew she was still mad and wanted to make it up to her and he knew for a fact that Leah's ear was a weak spot of hers.

"Mmmm," she moaned softly as she instantly started getting a pulse in her clitoris.

He was slowly disarming her as she started getting into the mood.

"No, no, no," she said, trying to get him to get up, but he was barely budging.

This nigga thinks he slick, she thought to herself. Leah was battling with trying to stand her ground about what happened yesterday. She didn't want Marcus to think that sex would be accepted as a form of apology, or could it?

He traced his tongue down her neck and she sucked her teeth. *Leah, you bet not fucking give into his stalking ass*, she coached herself. Marcus stood, picking Leah up with ease as he carried her over to the bed and arrested her arms so she couldn't resist him. "I'm sorry baby," he said, kissing her and then quickly moving to her right ear and then licked it slowly. The pulse in her clitoris became more intense and she couldn't help but be a willing participant in extracurricular activities that was about to take place. Marcus moved from Leah's ear down to her neck sucking so hard that it both hurt and felt good. *I know this nigga not putting a fucking hater mark on me*, she thought as she moved her neck from his grasp. Marcus snickered when Leah moved. "I see you don't want me marking you up." He then pulled her shirt up and lifted it over her head and attacked her right breast knowing her right side is the most sensitive.

Leah moaned as she squirmed and started pulling her pants down while he drove her crazy sucking on the right areola. Marcus had mastered her body over the summer and knew exactly what she liked and what she didn't. He rolled his tongue over to the left side giving that side a little attention as well. Leah pushed at his head making him go down south as she anticipated the warmth of his mouth reaching her southern lips. He kissed down her flat stomach slowly, dipping his tongue in her belly button and then tracing his tongue along the creases of her inner thighs as she spread her legs open wide. Marcus stuck one finger inside of Leah's wet walls and the way she clenched down on that one finger made his boy hard. *She is fucking drenching, damn*, Marcus thought to himself as he fingered her for several seconds before replacing his finger with his stiff tongue. As soon as Leah felt his tongue her whole body lifted from the bed as she moaned loudly.

"Dammit baby," she moaned as he pulled her back down and slid her more toward him. "Naw, don't run now bey, this what you wanted right? Take this shit like a big girl."

Leah let her legs fall to each side as she shoved his head into her pussy and grinded against his face.

"Just eat your damn lunch baby," she said with authority.

It was 12 in the afternoon, so she was serving up a special meal for him. Marcus circled his tongue over her entire pussy as she worked her hips, he was licking her shit like it would be his last lunch meal. "I'm sorry baby," he said in between

92

each lick. Leah didn't respond, she was too busy wanting to catch a spasm. Marcus jabbed that tongue in her pussy.

"I said I'm sorry," he moaned.

"Okay, baby Okayyyy," she squealed as Marcus started flicking his tongue against her clit faster and applying pressure as he did it. Leah was dripping wet and was ready to fuck. "Take your pants off baby," she said all while making sure he never took his mouth off her flesh as she moved her hips to a rhythm. Marcus reached up and started flicking at her nipples as he applied more pressure to the strokes he was giving her womanhood with his tongue. This had Leah spent as she felt her orgasm building and her legs started trembling.

"Wait, baby stop." Leah grasped Marcus by the ears, tugging him up and stared in his beautiful light brown eyes. "I want to cum all over that dick," she said. Leah was ready for him to penetrate her with his love stick. Marcus entered her dripping box and groaned in satisfaction as he stroked her clit while pumping in and out of her. He was enjoying the view as she was playing with her own nipples now and making herself even wetter from the sensation. Marcus then laid on top of her as she locked her legs around his waist.

"Damn, bey you soaked," he growled in her ear and then kissed it softly.

He was gassing Leah head up with so much confidence in her sexuality, she smirked slightly. Leah took him by surprise when she started matching him pump for pump. He was used to doing all the work when she was on the bottom. Leah fucking him back made him go crazy.

"Leah." He grunted.

Her sex had him feeling soft. She felt good. This sex with her wasn't normal, the feelings inside him weren't normal. He sucked his teeth and bit into his lip as he shook his head. Marcus had never experienced this emotion. The words that were forming at the tip of his tongue were threatening to escape. *Shit*, he thought.

"I fucking love you," he called out as he started picking up his pace.

Leah moans seized and her eyes filled with not only passion but with emotion as well. That statement had come out of nowhere, taking the air out of Leah's lungs. Did he mean it or was he just that into the bliss she was serving? Leah wasn't sure how to feel but her heart swelled as she picked up her pace.

"I love you too baby," she whispered back.

Marcus retreated from inside her, he wasn't ready for this ride to end. He lifted her right leg and started licking, up and down her thigh, sending chills through her body.

"Give her a kiss baby," Leah moaned as she caressed the top of his head.

Marcus licked his full lips and made his way to *her*. He wrapped his lips around her sex giving it one long suck, tasting her before he kissed it and then inserted his man back inside. Marcus hit her with a deep stroke and kissed her as he hit her with one more deep stroke causing her to cream all over him. "Agh," Leah cried out as her body went through different channels of pleasure. She rode the wave of ecstasy, enjoying every second.

"Fuck bey," Marcus said as he came hard inside of her, no pulling out and no thinking of the possible consequences of his actions by being caught in the moment since he slid up in her raw.

They laid there breathing heavy and exhausted because of the race they were just in to get to the finish line. Leah was on a sexual high that she didn't want to come down from. Marcus had depleted her and snatched all her self-discipline she was trying to hold onto. She had allowed his sex to become a form of apology and didn't care one bit because it was an excellent one. Marcus rolled over from off Leah and stretched his arm out so she could snuggle under him.

"I think I want a job," she stated as she rubbed his chest, glad that he didn't have hair on it.

Leah didn't like hairy chest boys and she was appreciative that he was one of the ones without it.

"That's cool, but what makes you want to work all of a sudden?" He asked.

"Well, I've been thinking about it all summer, I really want to start doing things for myself without having to ask my mommy for nothing."

Marcus looked at her and was confused. He didn't understand why she felt like she couldn't ask him for what she needed. He was her man and could provide for her. He wanted to provide for her. She never asked him for anything, which made him want to give her everything.

"I mean that's cool and all but I got you bey."

Leah stopped him mid-sentence. Sitting up she adjusted the sheets to cover her breast as she looked him in the eyes. She had realized she didn't know what *all* he did to make his money. They had laid around numerous of times talking, but never did his hustling come up. Leah would always see him selling different merchandise and wondered why.

"Marcus we never really talked about what all you do to get your money and I want to know."

"I'm a stick up kid and slang them thangs, that's all there is to it," he said ready to change the subject.

"Yeah okay just make sure you're being careful *stick up kid*," Leah shot back.

"You don't have to worry about me bey, I'm straight, but I'm glad you want to hustle to get your own bey, straight go getter," Marcus responded.

Marcus started kissing on Leah's neck as the thought of her wanting to be independent turned him on but cut the encounter short when his phone chimed. Marcus leaned over the side of the bed to retrieve the phone, he checked the alert and smirked. Leah noticed him grin and then quickly stuffed it back in his jeans. *This nigga phone sure has been rocking lately*, she thought to herself as he started to kiss on her again. She was no longer in the mood as her mind began to race at what the hell could be going on, first he seemed sneaky when she first walked in the room from brushing her teeth and now this.

"Listen I'm about to shower and get my day started," she said as she moved her face away from him.

He looked at her like he couldn't believe what he was hearing and caught an instant attitude.

"So, you just going to leave a nigga with blue balls?" he asked as he rubbed his pole against her. He was ready to try any and everything to get her soaked for him again.

"Um, yeah I am home skillet, I got stuff to do," Leah replied dismissing the conversation.

She stood from the bed and started preparing the things she needed for her shower. She didn't care one bit that he was still laying there, dick hard and attitude all over his face. As she finished her preparations, she looked at him and shook her head. "So, are you going to chillax or are you leaving, cause if you're leaving, I need to lock the door behind you real quick."

She started making her way to the bedroom door. Marcus was pissed, she was letting him leave with a hard dick and an attitude. To him, that shit was disrespectful. He had never had a chick deny him of sex or anything for that matter. Marcus thought about staying, hoping Leah would change her mind, but when he noticed her mood not changing as she stood and waited by the door, he said fuck it. "Yeah, imma bounce," he said climbing out of bed and dressing in haste. Leah held onto the doorknob as she waited for him to get his things. She knew he was livid. She could see it all over him. "I guess I'll hit you later," he said as he exited the bedroom and made his way to the front door.

Leah trailed behind him with her arms folded and a look of disgust on her face. Marcus turned to peck Leah on the cheek when they reached the front door. She wanted to move her face away, but she didn't. She let him peck her cheek and then make his exit without a word. Leah didn't know what it was, but she had a feeling that he was up to something. Her god mom had always told her to never go searching for things you are not prepared to find. So, Leah dismissed her negative thoughts and headed back to her bedroom to get in the shower. She wasn't prepared to find something that could possibly cause her heart ache. If Marcus was doing dirt she would sure find out and be sure to clean it up when the time came.

Leah showered and dressed in plain blue jeans with a casual button-down shirt to match with a white tank top underneath and all white K-Swiss. She pulled her hair up into a neat ponytail with bangs and looked at her reflection in the mirror, loving what she saw staring back at her. "I guess I'll make this a productive Friday," she said as she grabbed her purse and started making her way out the door. When she opened the front door, she jumped slightly dropping her house keys as Tyson was in mid knock.

"Dammit Ty, you scared the hell out of me," she shrieked as he kneeled, picking her keys up for her.

"My bad lor sis," he said, handing her keys over.

"What's poppin baller?" She said chuckling.

Tyson stood there wearing a blue jean Levi outfit with a black t-shirt underneath and all black Air-Forces on his feet and a gold chain with the letter *N* that hung from it. Leah knew that *N* stood for NuNu and she smiled at the way Tyson was repping her friend.

"It's all good, but what are you doing here Ty and what's lor?" She asked, confused as she closed the front door and locked it.

Tyson laughed, he always forgot he wasn't back home, so they didn't know the slang they used in Maryland. "My fault, I forget I'm not in B-More, but lor means little," he explained.

"Where are you heading, you need a ride?" He asked as they both started walking off the porch.

"Well, I wanted to go fill out a couple applications real quick," she replied. "Aight, I got you. Let's go, I need your help with a few things anyway, so we can roll and talk."

Leah hopped in the car wondering what he wanted help with, whatever it was she knew he was desperate if he wanted her help. It was a nice Friday afternoon. Leah rolled down her window letting the breeze blow through on her side.

"You know Nu birthday is in two weeks and I want to throw her a party and surprise her with a car," Tyson said as he steered with one hand and tried to flip through his cd case with the other.

"Boy, give me that you just drive and I'll DJ," Leah said, snatching the case away from him.

"Aight Leah, damn with your bossy ass," he said laughing. Leah laughed as well as she flipped through the case, picking out Jay-Z's cd. She popped it in and the first song that played was her cut. Leah started jamming before Tyson interrupted her vibe.

"What do you think about the party and the car idea?" He quizzed as he hit his turn signal to get over into the next lane.

"I mean the party is a great idea and the car thing I'd have to get with Ms. Andrea to see what she thinks," she said. Leah's brain started working as she started thinking of party themes. Then an idea clicked in her head. Her friend Tasha's uncle owned a nightclub that she was sure he would let them rent out for the night of the party. "Wait, Nu ass can't even drive so how the hell are you getting her a damn car Ty, she would hit some shit and tear it up all in the same day," Leah said laughing.

"Naw, my lor mama knows how to drive. I've been teaching her all summer and she finally got it," he shot back in NuNu's defense.

She couldn't believe that this conversation never came up between her and NuNu. The girls had been so distracted by the boys lately that they were missing time and Leah didn't like that feeling. Tyson noticed the look on Leah's face and was able to dissect her thoughts. "Don't trip you've been laid up with my dummy Marcus that's why you didn't know," he said with a smirk. Leah punched him in the arm, "boy shut up talking shit."

I wonder what the hell his stupid ass doing, she thought. She wished Tyson wouldn't have mentioned his name, she still wasn't feeling him at the moment.

"Aye," Tyson called out, yanking her out of her thoughts.

"My fault Ty, but we can start planning the party later or over the weekend, if that's okay with you."

"Yeah I'm fine with that lor sis, just make sure you respond to my text."

Leah looked at him in confusion as she checked her phone, realizing it was on silent and seeing the missed calls from him and her godmother.

"Yeah, I see that now, my phone is on silent."

"Oh you must of didn't want no interruptions while you and Marcus were going on half on baby," he said grinning.

"You and this half on baby shit is getting on my damn nerve Ty. Just cause you and Nu were playing house and now got a baby, don't be burning bread on me homie. Besides I'm on birth control, so it ain't no going half on a baby this way," she stated.

"Yeah ard," Tyson said, still grinning.

"Speaking of the baby, you happy ain't you?" Leah asked.

She remembered the day he had announced that NuNu was pregnant. Tyson's face was filled with so much adoration. Leah could feel the love and excitement radiating from him, she was certain everyone in the room could feel it. It was that strong.

"Yeah I am, Nu is something special and I'm grateful for sharing this experience with her. I'm grateful for her having a friend like you as well. You always ride for my lor mama and I respect it cause most girls are scandalous as hell, a perfect example is the shit y'all home girl pulled. I got to give you your props for being a trill friend to my baby."

He held out his hand for a fist bump and Leah did the same. Leah smiled as their fists connected and then Tyson's face became Mandy's for a split second. Leah snapped her eyes shut and then opened them again.

"Yo, you good?" Tyson asked, noticing the disturbed look on her face.

Leah nodded. She was bugging out again and had to get it together.

"Yeah I'm good Ty, but that's my sister, me and Nu have been friends since 5th grade we locked in for life."

"Fa sho," Tyson said as he pulled in Wendy's parking lot.

"I'm coming in with you a nigga hungry and I might as well get some food while I'm waiting," he said.

They both walked in and stood in line waiting to place orders and talk to someone about getting an application. Leah heard chatter coming from the back as she approached the counter with Tyson right behind her.

"They asses sound like a bunch of gossiping boppers," Leah whispered over her shoulder before she asked the cashier if the hiring manager was in.

Tyson shook his head and laughed, she and NuNu were definitely alike in a lot of ways.

"Daynice to the front," the cashier called over the microphone and then asked if Leah could step to the side to wait as she took Tyson's order.

The manager walked from the back and the cashier told her that Leah was looking for the hiring manager. Daynice approached Leah and asked if they could sit at the booth right behind them. After 30 minutes of talking and laughing Leah walked out with a job and a start date. She ran to Tyson's car excited and ready to share the news. She climbed into the car and all she heard was.

"Ty if my damn frosty is melted by the time you get back here we are going to have serious issues."

Leah laughed and took the phone from him.

"Girl calm yo pregnant ass down I'll make sure he grabs you a new one right now, stop being so damn moody," Leah said, trying to stop NuNu from fussing.

"Bye Leah didn't nobody ask you shit," NuNu shot back hanging up.

Leah and Tyson both laughed. NuNu was already mean but this pregnancy was going to make her the devil for sure.

"What are you going to do with her ass?" Leah asked, still laughing.

"Pay her evil ass no attention when she acts like that," Tyson said as he pulled through the drive-thru to order his lady another medium chocolate frosty.

He ordered the frosty, paid and then headed straight back to the crib. Leah and Tyson talked more about the party and her getting the job on their way. Leah decided to stay with them for the rest of the day, wanting to spend time with NuNu after finding out about the baby and that she could drive. That small milestone had made Leah feel like she was missing out on important things in her friend's life, so she wanted to do some bonding. They laid around talking and watching BET for the rest of the day.

2 weeks Later

*I*t was the night of NuNu's 19th birthday party as Leah prepared herself for the evening. She and Marcus had shopped for hours trying to find the perfect all black outfits for the party's theme. When Tyson had come to her asking for ideas, they both agreed on an all black attire theme. Leah wore a black v-cut dress that came mid-thigh and Marcus had accompanied her with an all black suit brought out the man in him. He had requested that she wear the braids that Janet

Jackson had in the movie Poetic Justice and she did as he asked. Marcus stepped in as he watched Leah add the finishing touches to her look by laying her baby hairs down and then adding earrings. She was beautiful. The way the dress hugged her hips made Marcus want to indulge in her before the party. *Calm down homie, we don't have time right now. We'll hit that shit later*, he coached.

"You look fine as hell bey," he stated as he entered the room completely. Leah smiled in the mirror and gave him a wink.

"You ready?" he asked as he stood behind her and wrapped his arms around her waist. "Yep, let's roll," Leah said as she turned and pecked his lips.

"You don't look half bad yourself," she said as she craned her neck back while pulling at his suit jacket.

"Yeah, ya man do look good, don't I?" he said as he swiped a hand down his face.

Leah rolled her eyes.

"Alright now you can calm down homie you not all that," she said playfully.

They made their way to the party and pulled up at the same time as Tyson and NuNu. NuNu stepped out of the car in a black and gold one strap dress. The dress showed every single curve NuNu had and revealed her small baby bump. Her hair was bone straight with a middle part and her high yellow skin was glowing. Tyson was by her side with an all black suit on, with a gold shirt underneath. Tyson had paid his old school homie to use his night club for the event instead of who Leah had suggested, and he held back no expense. The couples stepped in the club and NuNu's mouth dropped. The club had black and gold balloons everywhere, black covered tables had been set with gold candles on top, and a live DJ in the booth. "Happy Birthday to our girl Nu'Asia," the DJ announced as Tyson gave him a head nod. The club was already packed with guests who were invited and NuNu couldn't believe her eyes. She had to blink away tears as she wiped at the corner of each eye.

"Ty, you didn't have to do all this," she said, turning to him.

Tyson leaned down and kissed her, "I know ma, but I wanted to."

NuNu stood on her tip toes as she kissed him again and then whispered in his ear, "we're doing some serious fucking when we get home."

"Indeed," he said with a smirk as he led her to the dance floor.

Leah and Marcus trailed behind the couple as they made their way to the dance floor. Leah tapped NuNu on the shoulder. "Leah Booo," NuNu said dramatically. "Happy Birthday baby," Leah said, closing the space in between them and taking NuNu in for a hug. NuNu meant everything to Leah and she was ready to celebrate yet another special birthday with her sister. They had a long night ahead of them and she hoped NuNu was ready to have a great night because Tyson had indeed out done himself. She held onto NuNu as they hugged, she looked ahead at the DJ's booth and saw an image of Mandy standing next to him, naked with bolts going through her body. Leah jumped causing the girls to part for a brief moment.

"You ard?" NuNu asked as she stepped back, looking puzzled. Leah still staring straight ahead nodded. She closed her eyes and took a deep breath.

"Yeah, boo I'm fine," she said plastering on a fake smile.

"I see Ty got your ass talking like him," Leah said laughing after realizing NuNu had used *ard* instead of aight.

Leah took a step back, looking NuNu up and down. NuNu looked amazing, pregnant belly and all. "You are rocking that dress Nu," she said, taking another step back and then stuck her tongue out. NuNu smiled and stuck her tongue out as well. She knew she was popping because she had spent a lot of time putting herself together for the night. Tyson tapped her, grasping her attention with the set of keys he was holding out. NuNu's mouth hit the floor,

"Ty, what are these for?" she asked, taking them from his grasp.

"Your black and pink Cuttie that's sitting outside, ma," he replied with a wink.

"Ayyye," NuNu screamed as she jumped up into his arms.

Tyson caught her effortlessly, bear hugging her but not too tight.

"I freaking love you Ty, thanks baby," she whispered.

Tyson kissed the side of her neck before placing her back down on her feet.

"No, thank you, ma. Thank you for being love and showing me love. I love you more lor mama."

NuNu leaned up and kissed him sensually, she loved this boy and everything about him.

She would have never envisioned in her life to end up with him. This was the type of fantasy that she saw playout on T.V. as a young teen. That Corey and Topanga from *Boy Meets World* type fantasy, but here she was living the vision and she was loving every second. NuNu pulled back from their kiss and snatched Leah by the hand and dragged her outside to see her new car. Tyson and Marcus swaggered behind the girls.

"You a sucka," Marcus said laughing as he slapped Tyson on the shoulder playfully. "Nah, you're a dummy," Tyson shot back.

As they stepped into the parking lot, one of Tyson's boys climbed out of the driver seat and handed Tyson the spare keys.

NuNu squealed in excitement as she climbed in the driver seat and Leah in the passenger. She was becoming emotional as tears started pooling in her eyes. It didn't help that she was pregnant, and her hormones were all over the place. Tyson, as usual sensed the emotions and gravitated toward her. He kneeled in front of her, cuffing her hands inside of his. He looked at her and his look told her that he needed to know her thoughts. They were that in tune with each other that they were able to communicate through looks alone.

"Ty, you've made this the best birthday ever," she said as she began to cry. She couldn't keep the tears back any longer. They rained down over her pretty face and Tyson stood and pulled her out of the car.

"Stop crying ma, you deserve everything you have been giving," he said, clearing the tears from her face.

He kissed her and in return, she stuck her tongue in his mouth. NuNu appreciated him and she was ready for the night to end so she could show him just how much she appreciated him.

"I'm ready to go Ty," she said in a seductive tone.

Tyson smiled. He knew when her voice got like that, she was ready to play house.

"Nu, what about the party ma?" He asked, chuckling at her eagerness.

"Ty, the party was cute, thank you but this kitty puurringg and I'm ready to let out a few meows," NuNu said, kissing him deeply while sliding her hand down to the seat of his slacks. Tyson groaned and lost all restraints.

"That's why your ass pregnant now," Leah called from the other side of the car.

"Girl shut the hell up and get out," NuNu said.

She gave Tyson one last peck and whispered in his ear to meet her at home. She was ready to come out of her clothes and show him her birthday suit.

"Nu, what about the party?" Leah asked as she climbed out the car in irritation.

"I'm finishing the party at home Leah damn. Now get out because I got shit to do." She said dismissively.

"Come on bey let's shake," Marcus said as he approached Tyson and dapped him up. "Aight Dummy, I'll rap with you later."

CHAPTER TEN

☐

Two months later

$\mathcal{T}$he girls were now a month into their senior year.

Leah was getting into the swing of balancing both a job and school. She was focused, determined to finish her senior strong and with no complications. She sat at work waiting for Marcus to pick her up while doing her accounting homework and messaging NuNu back and forth.

My Nu: If it's a boy I'm naming him Tyson JuRell Wilson Jr.

Leah: Ugh NO Nu, name him Emir Jurell Wilson

My Nu: Is this yo baby or mine Leah? Shit, I'm naming him after Ty

Leah: Whatever Nu let me see where the fuck Marcus black ass at he late

Leah dialed Marcus's number and right before she pressed the talk button he walked in smiling. Seeing him smile pissed her off. He had the nerve to walk in her job smiling as if he didn't just have her waiting for almost an hour.

"I don't know what the fuck you smiling at with your Danny Glover looking ass, you late," she spat.

Marcus laughed, approaching her booth and started helping get her books together.

"Aye, you can chill with trying to crack bey before I light yo ass up," he stated as he slid the bag on his left shoulder.

"Marcus I'm serious, why the hell are you so late? I've been off for almost an hour," she pouted.

"Man bey, Shan Shan left his little bitch in the basement at the crib, so I had to go get her for him before his mom dukes got home."

"Yeah whatever," she said as she snatched her book bag from off his shoulder and headed for the door.

When Leah approached the car she saw a girl climbing over the seat to get in the backseat. Leah yanked her door open, "Didn't anyone teach you not to climb over people's seats? That's mad disrespectful." she questioned beyond irritated as she hopped in the front seat and then turned to face the girl. *She's dusty as fuck*, Leah thought as she looked the girl up and down. The girl just sat there staring out the window. Leah rolled her eyes as she got comfortable and flipped through the cd case trying to find something that would calm her nerves. *I'm not going to let this bitch piss me off even more with her dirty ass*, Leah mumbled. She found a mix cd that had random written across it and popped that in.

Where would I be
Without you baby
So if you need me
If you want me
To put it on you

110

When Leah heard the song by JaRule and Lil Mo pump through the speakers she instantly got hype. "This is my song," she squealed as she cut the volume up and started rocking her head from side to side, singing right along with the song

Where would I be without my baby
The thought alone might break me
And I don't want to go crazy
But every thug needs a lady

Leah was truly in her own world as she sang the words to the song. Marcus just looked at her thinking she was trying to be funny with all the singing and dancing. The girl sat in the backseat smiling. She had one up and Leah. *This bitch trying to be funny, but only if she knew*, the girl thought. Leah was oblivious to what was going on. She trusted her man, she simply thought that this girl was just some random ho that one of his boys smashed and then left behind. They pulled up in front of her house and Leah cut the radio down confused.

"What are we pulling up here for?" she asked.

"What you mean I'm dropping you off," he said as he got out of the car.

Leah rolled skeptical eyes at Marcus as she grabbed her book bag, opened her door and then slammed it shut. Marcus walked toward Leah, taking the book bag from her, as he instructed her to walk in front of him. She didn't know what was going on, but something was telling her that her man was up to something. An alarm was going off within her that she just could not ignore. First, he was almost an hour late picking her up and now he was dropping her off while he still had some girl in the car. *This muthafucka up to something*, she thought to herself. It was no way he was dropping her off and then rolling around the city with the next bitch acting as a taxi. One thing Leah knew for sure is Marcus didn't extend rides to no one. She had heard him telling his own sister that she couldn't get a ride down the street to the gas station.

Leah wanted to bite her tongue and give her man the benefit of the doubt. Her mind was at war with her heart at the moment. Marcus was her man, he wouldn't lie. *He said it was Shan Shan's bitch, he wouldn't play me like that, he ain't that damn bold.* Leah headed up the driveway dismissing her thought's. She would take his word, this time. Leah reached the first step to her porch and stopped abruptly, a nagging feeling came over her. Woman's intuition. Leah had never experienced this before and it was pushing her to speak up about the girl in the car.

"Marcus, what you got going on?" Leah asked.

She didn't yell, she didn't give attitude, she just simply asked him a question hoping that she knew him as well as she thought she did.

"Nothing bey damn," before he could even finish his lie she snatched her book bag telling him she didn't even care.

Leah walked to the door with Marcus on her heels. He was lying and she knew it deep down inside. How he answered the question had said a lot without him admitting to what the truth was. However, Leah couldn't prove it. What was she going to do, go back to the car and ask the girl was she fucking her man? Nah, her pride wouldn't allow it. She didn't want to give the next chic that type of satisfaction.

"Marcus just go and drop Shan bitch off," she said softly.

"Man, what is up? Why you trippin?" He said.

"Nigga, did I tell you I wanted to come tonight? NO, and now all of sudden you dropping me off cause this bitch in the car?" She yelled.

She tried to let it go, but Marcus wouldn't allow her. She never wanted to let the next bitch see her sweat. That was one thing her god mother had taught her. Yet her teachings were non-existent right now because Leah was doing the complete opposite.

"Leah you tripping, I'ma drop her off and then come back and swoop you after you shower and get out of them greasy ass work clothes."

"Naw, dawg I'm good I'll stay here," she said unlocking the door and going in without another word.

Marcus returned to the car feeling fucked up inside. What he thought was player, actually made him feel like a scum. *What the fuck was I thinking bringing this bitch with me?* he thought. He knew he was wrong, but he would never tell her that he had just smashed another bitch. Marcus was bold, but admitting to something like that, he knew would ruin Leah. She loved him and would do anything he asked, he was certain. She had proved that to him over the summer. However, being with just one girl he wasn't ready to do. Marcus had been rocking with Chrissy way before he met Leah. Leaving her alone would be hard for him to do. He had tried numerous times, failing each time miserably. He would creep with her while Leah worked and then turn his phone off once Leah was in his presence at night. Marcus got back in his car as Chrissy climbed back over his seats, retrieving her original spot. Marcus stared at the girl, shaking his head.

"Yo Chrissy, that was some foul shit I just pulled," Marcus said as he started the engine.

Chrissy laughed. She didn't care not one bit, why should she? She had wanted to lay eyes on the bitch that was taking her spot and spend one last night with who was supposed to be her man only. Sparing Leah's feelings was the least of her concerns. Who was sparing her feelings? She would have to move on from the boy that she spent the last five months with. Marcus was cutting her off for a bitch that she never even heard of before.

"Oh well, it's over now. Just take me out like we agreed, and you won't have to worry about being foul from this day forward. At least not with me anyway." Chrissy said dismissing the conversation.

Marcus shook his head, shrugged his shoulders and drove off. *Fuck it.*

*E*ntering the house, Leah went straight to the kitchen following the smell of chicken, wafting through the air.

"What's crackin g mommy?" Leah said walking in the kitchen and sitting her bag down.

"Hey baby, what are you doing here, especially on the weekend?" Stacy asked as she dropped a batch of chicken in the grease.

"I don't even want to get into it mommy," Leah stated.

How could she tell her god mom that she thought Marcus was cheating on her? Stacy would let her have it about what had just occurred outside. Leah didn't want to bring her into her and Marcus's problems. She opted to keep it to herself and just figure it out on her own. Stacy looked at her god daughter with skeptical eyes. She noticed Leah's mood and knew that her and Marcus must have had some kind of argument. However, they were young and it was expected. She wouldn't pry into their teenage drama. Leah was 18, a grown woman. She would let her start to figure things out on her own, stepping in only if necessary.

"Leah, your mom came by today, she said you hadn't been answering her calls," Stacy said as she flipped the chicken.

She knew how Leah felt about her mother and the things that had taken place however, Lena was still her friend which meant she wanted things between her and Leah to be hashed out.

"G mommy, you know that woman only coming around now that I'm grown. I haven't heard from her in 3 years, now all of a sudden I'm 5 months away from my 19th birthday and now she's calling and coming around. Naw, I'm good, I don't want to speak not a word to her," Leah said, getting emotional.

The day was turning out to be awful and now Leah was losing all control.

"What kind of woman allows a man to stay in the home after his grown ass son rapes her daughter HUH?"

Leah was crying at this point at the thought of the trauma she endured when she was 11. Stacy cut the grease off, not caring that chicken was still frying. She headed straight to Leah pulling her up and wrapping her in a hug.

"Oh, baby girl it's okay," Stacy said soothingly while placing Leah head on her shoulder and rubbing her back.

"But it's not though mama, I barely sleep at night and I think of what happened all the time," Leah said while shaking her head.

Stacy grasped Leah by the arm leading the way to the living room. She took a seat in the corner of the couch. Leah laid across it laying her head in her lap, as Stacy rubbed her head.

"Leah, you never told me you were uncomfortable with that boy daddy still staying there," Stacy said. "I would have taken you sooner had I known all this."

Leah cried, uncontrollably, the memory always haunted her. It confused her often on why her mother would allow her rapist father to remain in their home after what his son did. How was Lena able to still lay in bed with the man that raised that type of boy? Did she not think that it could have been learned behavior? Did she not consider how Leah might feel about looking at the man with the same face as her perpetrator? All these questions skipped through Leah's mind constantly, like a scratched up CD.

"G mommy I've always been scared of that man, a little before what happened and even more after it happened."

116

Leah cried as her chest heaved. Stacy looked down at her daughter with an aching heart. She never knew that Leah was at war with these things within herself. How did she miss the signs? She would hear Leah up at night but never questioned it. *What type of god mother am I?* she thought. Stacy wiped at Leah's face.

"Leah, baby, you should have been said something, you know I don't play that shit when it comes to you, YOU KNOW THIS," Stacy said. "Remember when he whooped you when you were a little girl and you called me about it." Leah chuckled a little remembering that day she called her godmother after her mom's boyfriend had whopped her. She wiped at her face, sniffing.

"Yeah I remember," she said with a smile.

"You came around that corner so fast with a bat swinging."

"That's right," Stacy said laughing at the memory herself.

"I was about to remove his black ass head off his shoulders over my baby. Me and your mom didn't talk for a couple of weeks after that and she kept me away from you over it but for you, it was worth it. Leah, don't ever keep stuff in and not tell me, you know we're better than that."

Leah's phone began ringing while she and Stacy continued to talk. She ignored it needing every moment of this time with her god mom. Her phone rang again.

"Ugh, hold on mommy, let me make sure this ain't Nu calling back to back like this," she said as she lifted from the couch to fetch her phone.

Leah grabbed her phone from her bookbag and answered.

"Hello,"

117

NuNu was yelling. Leah could barely understand what she was saying.

"Wait, what's wrong Nu? You okay?" Leah asked in alarm.

She listened as NuNu spoke, confused.

"Nu, how you picking me," she said, shaking her head.

Leah knew she had to be joking. It was no one way NuNu was driving. NuNu could barely drive at night, so she always had Tyson drive her places when it got late.

"You took Ty's car, Nu what the hell?" She asked.

"Okay, okay, I'm getting ready now."

Leah hung up the phone. NuNu had said three words to let her know that it was about to be some stuff going down. Leah didn't know what exactly was going on but hearing NuNu say put sweats, sneakers, and grab the vaseline was all she needed to hear. She would get the details on the way.

"That was Nu mommy I'll be back," Leah said running to her room.

She took off her work clothes, threw on a pair of Apple Bottom valor sweats, a plain black t-shirt, and all black air force ones. Leah then threw her hair into a ponytail, grabbed the vaseline off her dresser and headed out the house.

Leah hopped in Tyson's all red old skool *88* Buick regal that sat on 20in rims. "Nu who the hell your pregnant ass think you're about to fight?" Leah said as she started putting the vaseline on her face. That was her and NuNu's ritual when it came to them getting down, it would make it hard for the other person to scratch their faces. Other hoes wind milled and scratched all the damn time but not them, they were rough and threw hands like they were boys.

118

"Leah, listen Tasha just called me and said she saw Marcus with some bitch in the club all over each other, bumping and grinding like it's nobody's business," NuNu said as she hit her blinker to turn right onto Sylvania Ave.

Vamps nightclub was 10 minutes away from her house but NuNu cut that drive down to 5. Leah's mind was racing. She couldn't fucking believe what she was hearing. *I just know this nigga not playing me like a shorty*, she thought.

"Nu, is Tasha sure it was him?" she asked.

Leah wanted to be sure. Hell, she wanted to be more than sure, because there was no way he was at a club with a bitch. Marcus had just left her house just an hour ago. *This day just couldn't get any worse,* she thought as NuNu pulled in the parking lot of the night club carelessly.

"Nu, be careful parking this boy car or he for sure going to have a fit," Leah said holding onto the door.

"Girl, Tyson doesn't run anything but his mouth, I run him, let's not get that fact twisted," NuNu said smiling.

"Anyways," Leah said, rolling her eyes as they both hopped out of the car.

"Nu, you better not jump in, I got this, it's bad enough you out here while you're pregnant," Leah stated.

"Girl, I don't want to hear that shit right now," NuNu shot back.

They entered the building with ease bypassing the others waiting in line since Tasha's uncle was the one who owned the club. Tasha was already by the door waiting. The music was bumping, and lights were flashing different colors throughout the building. The club was poppin for sure. Leah had wished they were there under different circumstances, because now that they were, she wanted to kick it.

NuNu spotted Marcus and the girl on the dance floor rocking to Lil Jon and the EastsideBoyz new song *BIA BIA*. NuNu tapped Leah.

"There he is," she said pointing in his direction.

Leah squinted and started heading to the dance floor to act a fool. Here was Marcus black ass on the dance floor with the same bitch he claimed was Shan Shan bopper. *This lying ass nigga,* she thought.

"Girl, that's Chrissy ole trout mouth ass that he is with," NuNu said.

Leah stopped and started nodding her head, she was going to do this shit right. NuNu, was confused at what the hell her friend was doing but without question, she started nodding as well. Chyna White's verse of the song came on and the two girls started rocking to her part, rubbing their hands together like they were one of the boys, getting in each other's face moving side to side. Leah nodded in Marcus and the girl's direction and NuNu followed suit as they kept their same movements going but were making their way over to them. Marcus and the girl weren't aware of their surroundings as Leah said *"Leah a thug bitch with no feelings inside"* making the artist words her own in that moment as she bumped the chic Marcus was with. Chrissy caught her balance and then thought she saw a ghost when she saw Leah's face.

"Yeah, bitch," Leah barked as she swung on her, punching her straight in the mouth.

"Bitch you thought I wouldn't find out," Leah roared as she was laying hands all over the girl's face.

Chrissy tried to grab Leah by the hair but was unsuccessful.

"Should have been quicker on your feet hoe," Leah spat as she wrapped Chrissy's ponytail around her fist, cocking the other one back to deliver a blow to her face.

Marcus knew he had fucked because he stood there. He didn't know what to do. Leah was beating the breaks off of Chrissy's ass as NuNu stood off to the side with a crowd of partiers watching, making sure no one jumped in. She noticed one girl looking like she wanted parts

"Aye, this not even yo beef boo, let my girl get her round, cause trust me the bitches connected to each one of my wrists you don't want to meet," NuNu announced to the girl, wanting her to jump bad. NuNu wanted Chrissy's friend to give her a reason to rock her ass real quick. The girl crossed the dance floor in irritation and NuNu went back to cheering Leah on as she continued rocking Chrissy's boppin ass.

"Stomp her ass, Leah!" NuNu shouted as she clapped her hands together.

Marcus went to pull Leah off the girl but then he felt a shove from his right side.

"Don't fucking touch her you sorry ass nigga," NuNu yelled.

She never liked Marcus and didn't see what Leah saw in him. She wanted better for her friend and hoped that this would be the end of them. NuNu had every intention of calling Tyson if he even flinched at her.

A bouncer came across the dance floor as the music was stopped and grabbed Leah up from off Chrissy. Leah was over the bouncer's shoulder talking shit with tears falling as she was carried out the club. NuNu was right behind her but not before she kicked Chrissy ass in the stomach just for GP.

"Nu, get me the fuck out of here," Leah cried as the bouncer placed her on her feet. They headed towards Tyson's car.

"Come on, Nu please," Leah said, snatching on the handle of the car door.

"Okay boo, okay I'm hurrying," NuNu replied as she quickened her steps to hurry up and unlock the car doors.

NuNu popped the locks and right before Leah went to open the door she folded over, vomiting. NuNu closed the driver's side door and rounded the car to comfort her. She pulled Leah's hair back while rubbing her back.

"Let it out baby," she said, "it's okay." Leah was a mess as she continued to puke up everything in her stomach.

"I can't fucking believe this nigga," she cried wiping her mouth after she was finished.

"Leah you don't need him, fuck him and Chrissy dusty feet ass," NuNu said with sympathy.

Leah leaned against the car, defeated. The day was one emotional day and Leah had no energy left in her. She couldn't believe that her man had turned out to be one dog ass nigga. Here she was standing outside with her heart shattered and Marcus still in the club leaving her to pick up the pieces on her own.

"His ass still in the club with this bitch," Leah said as she slid to the ground.

"No, no, that's what we are not going to do Leah," NuNu said as she lifted her friend from the ground.

"Get up and let's go now, you not about to let these bums see you sweat or cry over no nigga. Come on," NuNu said opening the passenger side door for Leah to climb in.

Leah got in and before she got to shut the door her mouth started watering and the contents of her stomach came up again. Luckily she was quick and opened the door wide so it wouldn't get all over Tyson's car. This time NuNu got in the car as she waited for her to stop throwing up. Leah's heart was broken and she couldn't wrap her mind around the fact that Marcus still hadn't brought his stupid ass out of the club. *He doesn't care,* Leah thought. She spit the remaining fluid from her mouth as she closed the door and leaned the seat back. Leah was hot. She rolled the window down as she tried to let air flow through the window to cool her down. *I can't believe this muthafucka.*

"You can pull off. I'm ready to go home, shower and go to bed Nu."

"Okay boo I gotchu," NuNu replied as she pulled out of the parking lot and into traffic. NuNu's phone started ringing and she had Leah answer.

"Leah where's my baby mama at?" Tyson asked.

"She's right here Ty, she's dropping me off and then heading home," Leah responded in a low tone.

She now had a headache and wished she would have never come up to the club.

"Okay, tell her I'm on her head for taking my car to take yo ass to knock some bitch out." He shot back.

"Ty we both know you not going to do nothing to her, so stop it." Leah chuckled.

"You right, but didn't nobody ask you, Leah tell my baby to hurry," Tyson said hanging up.

Leah looked over to NuNu, "Ty said hurry up Nu, he misses you."

"Girl I know he was talking shit and then changed his tune when you said y'all both know he is not going to do nothing." Leah laughed slightly knowing NuNu knew her man all too well.

"Yeah, you right but how does he know what we were doing if he was sleeping when you left?" Leah quizzed.

As if they could read each other's mind they both said at the same time looking at each other, MARCUS.

□

CHAPTER ELEVEN

"*Yo*, bitch gonna give me a second round when I catch her," Chrissy said as Marcus pulled in front of her house. "That bitch went in my pockets and took my ID and money before the bouncer pulled her up and I want my shit back."

"Man, Chrissy, I got to make a move and I'm not trying to argue," Marcus stated. Chrissy looked at him agitated. She couldn't believe he was playing her to the left. She climbed out the car defeated and Marcus pulled off racing to Leah's. He had warned Chrissy that Leah would press it to her, but she insisted on seeing who had his heart. Marcus couldn't help but laugh at the thought. He knew Leah was savage but didn't know she was a savage like that. His and Chrissy's conversation played in his head until he reached Leah's street and parked. Marcus knew he fucked up, realizing he didn't know how he was going to explain anything. *Why did I do that dumb ass shit*, he thought as he turned the ignition back on and pulled away. He decided that it would be better to let things die down and then come back and talk to her.

Leah heard Marcus pulling up from the bass of his loudspeakers. She watched him from the window until he pulled away from her house without getting out. The sight of him leaving made her sick all over again as she rushed to the kitchen sink throwing up her entire insides. "Ugh, what the fuck is wrong with me?" She cried after she finished, heading to the bathroom to brush her teeth. While brushing her teeth she remembered that she had gone in Chrissy's pockets and took her ID.

Leah hurried and finished brushing her teeth, shut the water off, and placed her toothbrush in the holder. She headed to her bedroom where she had peeled out of her clothes and went into her sweats to retrieve Chrissy's belongings. Leah pulled the ID out and 25 dollars along with it. "Broke bitch," Leah said in disgust as she threw the money on her bed. She looked at the ID wondering if she should call NuNu up and her take her to this bitch's crib. *You know what? Fuck this shit*, she thought pulling out her phone to call a cab.

When the cab arrived and notified Leah, she headed out the door. She climbed in, running off the address to her destination and sat back. Her mind was racing because she was ready to fuck some shit up. How Marcus could be so bogus and have another bitch in the car with him while he picked his main girl up was beyond her. Leah laughed to herself thinking about how the girl wouldn't even look at her in the car and how when she popped up at the club the girl looked like she was ready to run out of there. "*Ole scary ass bitch*," she laughed to herself. *I'm fucking this nigga up too, for staying in the fucking club with this muskrat looking ass bitch*, she thought.

She leaned her head against the window and stared out of it. All of a sudden she felt as if someone was staring at her. A chill came over her as if the cabbie had the air conditioner on

126

full blast. She glanced at the rearview mirror and Mandy's image was sitting next to her. Leah scurried against the door, screaming as she shut her eyes with quickness and covered her mouth. The driver was slightly startled as he peered back at her through the rearview mirror.

"Ma'am is everything okay back there?"

"Yes, everything is fine. How much longer?" Leah asked with her eyes still shut tightly.

She couldn't open them. She was afraid of the image that would be peering back at her. Leah needed to get out of the cab and fast. She was freaking out and she knew she looked crazy.

"We will be arriving in 2 minutes ma'am. Are you sure you're fine?" The cabbie asked again for reassurance.

She took a deep breath, releasing it slowly, and nodded. She was tripping and she knew it.

"Get it together Leah," she said, her voice barely audible.

When they arrived at her destination Leah opened her eyes slowly peering to her left and sighed. She pulled her wallet out of her purse, "How much?" she asked as she flipped through the bills in her wallet.

"That'll be 19.86," the cabbie called out.

Leah handed him a 20 and exited the car. She stood outside of the home for about 10 minutes trying to figure out if she made the right choice by popping up. She walked up the long driveway and went around to the side door. She started to knock but stopped and twisted the knob instead, letting herself in and heading straight to the basement. Walking into the backroom she found Marcus laying in his bed sleeping. She stood in the doorway arms folded across her chest watching him for a moment. "I should fucking slap the fuck out of him," she whispered as she started making her way to his bed. He looked a little bit too peaceful for her liking and before she knew it, she swung on his ass connecting her fist right with his jaw.

BOP

"Get yo sorry ass up," she screamed as she hit him again this time socking him in the eye. Marcus shot up pissed and holding his eye as he tried to restrain her from throwing more blows his way.

"Leah, chill the fuck out," he said as he stood behind her, bear hugging her.

Leah was enraged. He had hurt her and then had the nerve to not come and talk it out with her. Seeing him sleeping so comfortable as if he had not one worry of losing her, pissed Leah off. Her man was a cheater but yet she wanted him, she craved him.

"Fuck you, Marcus!" She shouted as she tried to free herself from his tight hold.

"Let me the fuck go *NOW*, Marcus before I-"

"Before you what? Go in my pockets like you did ole girl," he said chuckling at the thought.

He loved the thought of Leah being able to handle her own. She was aggressive and he relished in the thought of her being with catching heat behind him.

"Leah, you savage as fuck, you know that." Marcus leaned into her attempting to kiss her ear. He knew that was her weak spot and he needed her to calm down. Just as his lips were getting ready to connect to her earlobe, she moved her head forward. "Don't fucking put your nasty as lips on me," she said as she elbowed him in his side freeing herself. Marcus leaned over holding his side and winced.

"Leah! Man, you got one more time to put your fucking hands on me," he barked.

"You broke my heart you bitch ass nigga, so I'm going to lay hands where I fucking please and if I want to lay them on you that's exactly where they going to land."

Marcus stood up straight, grabbing her by the waist and pulling her in. He needed to subdue her. He needed to get her to let her guard down and forgive him. Marcus had scolded himself the whole ride home after pulling from in front of her house. He knew his actions were stupid and mad disrespectful.

"I fucked up bey, I know," he whispered.

"You damn right you fucked up," she shot back. Leah began to cry. She was now depleted. Here she was trying to be the roots of Marcus's tree while he was busy wanting the leaves that would eventually fall.

"You know the shit I've been through and the things I've seen and for you to play me like this after you said you got me, is hurtful. I never expected this shit from you, Marcus. Where did I go wrong?"

At that very moment, Marcus knew he had her locked in and he used her vulnerability to his advantage to get her to stay right where he wanted her and that was with him. He was certain she wouldn't leave. Marcus looked her in the eyes and rubbed her cheek.

"I'm not ready to settle down, I can't just fuck one girl, I mean I can try but that's only if you stay down with a nigga," he said challenging her. Marcus needed to see if Leah was

129

going to be his rider. He wanted her to be like Chrissy, go with the flow and willing to accept whatever he dished out. He hoped that his plan to get her to submit would work. Leah recoiled at what she was hearing. Marcus had lost his mind. Stay down for what? To be disrespected and feel worthless.

"What the fuck you mean you'll try if I stay? Are you crazy?" She asked in disbelief.

"Listen either you with me or you, not, either way, I'm going to do me and since you not sure if you with me then you can get the fuck out until you figure it out."

Leah's eyes couldn't stop replenishing tears as she tried to process how he went from her mister charming to a typical dawg ass nigga. Marcus sauntered over to his bedroom door and opened it knowing she wouldn't leave and that she would fall for his game. Leah looked at him with shocked eyes, mouth agape.

"Wow."

Leah swiped the tears from her cheeks and walked right past him as she made her exit. Marcus was caught off guard by her actions. This is not how he planned for it to go. He was certain she would stay. Leah making her exit, instead of caving for him put something on him. He loved this girl but wasn't ready to settle down. Selfish. Marcus was selfish because he still wanted her to stay and put up with his bullshit, while he sorted through his mess. Marcus wanted to stop her. Something was telling him to stop her, but he let her walk right out the door without a word. His ego caused him to let his love leave. Leah walked back out the same way she came as she dialed NuNu up. As soon as her friend answered she asked her to come and get her from the gas station that was right up the street from Marcus's house. She walked down the long driveway, then looked back at the house as she shook her head. *I'm cool on that nigga.*

hree weeks had gone by since Leah and Marcus had last seen or spoken to each other. He never reached out like she thought he would and that cut her deeply. Leah was spending a lot of time at work, school and with NuNu. NuNu was getting bigger by the day but she still went to school and on days she couldn't make it, Leah would collect her work she needed and then return it if NuNu needed her to. Luckily for NuNu, she had all the credits she needed to graduate so being pregnant didn't set her back school wise, she just hoped she would be able to attend her prom as she and Leah had always planned.

Leah walked in NuNu's house from school and when she entered, she was taken aback by the face she saw staring at her.

"What's up bossy?" Tyson asked as he stood to take the extra book bag from her hand. "Hey Ty," she said as she finally took her eyes off Marcus.

"Ty, can you run me to the store real quick please?" Leah asked.

131

She didn't wait for a response. Leah was heading back toward the door until Marcus's comment stopped her.

"I'll take you," He said, standing up from the rocking chair he and Tyson had just put together for NuNu. Leah spun back around.

"Naw, you good Mr. I can't just fuck one bitch."

Leah didn't know what made Marcus think she'd just be willing to ride with him. They hadn't spoken in weeks and here he was having the nerve to want to offer her a ride after he had kicked her out and had come at her with the craziest ultimatum. Leah scoffed.

"Ty, I'll be at your car," she said, turning to him and then heading out the door.

"Okay, sis here I come," he said heading to the kitchen to grab his keys off the counter.

Marcus headed out the house catching up to Leah before she got to the sidewalk and grabbed her hand. "Leah, so this what we on?" he asked, turning her to face him.

When she turned around tears were falling as she nodded and then headed for the car after snatching out of his grasp. Marcus remained on the sidewalk until Tyson came out of the house. Tyson walked past Marcus who was now on his phone and tossed Leah the keys so that she could unlock the doors. Leah popped the locks and climbed in. She didn't know what he expected. Marcus had left her heart stomped on in his mother's basement. She wasn't willing to turn a cheek to his bullshit. He was willing to allow another bitch to ride shotgun and she wasn't coming second to no one. Tyson made his way to the driver's side climbing in as he yelled to

Marcus that he'd get back up with him later. Tyson then shut the door and before he started the engine Leah stopped him.

"What? I thought you wanted to go to the store."

"No, I just wanted him to leave and I knew he wouldn't stay if you left cause he knows Nu don't like his ass."

Tyson shook his head laughing at her cause she was right, NuNu couldn't stand Marcus. She would always give him attitude anytime he would have him around and talk mad shit about how she was glad Leah had left his ugly, cheating ass alone.

"But for real Ty, when did y'all get all buddy-buddy?"

"Leah, I've been known him from around the way. Him and I do business and get to this money. I can't let what y'all got going on disrupt my money flow, I had to tell Nu the same thing," he said.

Leah folded her arms and rolled her eyes as she threw her head against the headrest slightly. Seeing Marcus's face had ruined her day. His presence was one she wanted to avoid for as long as she could. Since that night in his basement, she had been broken. It was no way that she could ever forgive him. *I can't just fuck one bitch*, Leah scoffed as his words played back in her head.

"Ty, you know Nu got that in check," Leah said, smiling.

Tyson smirked. NuNu was his weakness. That was something everyone knew and something he would never deny. However, when it came to his money, it was a different story unless it would bring her harm in any way. Other than that, NuNu didn't dictate his business.

133

"She may run a lot of things, but one thing she doesn't run is the way I get my money, that's one thing she will *never* be able to control."

Leah smiled knowing why he put so much force behind that never.

"Okay brother, I can respect it, but for future references when you know I'm on my way can you at least give me a heads up and I'll wait until y'all done before I come over here."

"I got you."

They both exited the car and headed back in the house. Leah was ready to be up under her friend. She needed NuNu to make her laugh and get her mind off her now reopened wound.

"Nuuuu," Leah called out, being dramatic.

"What?" NuNu shouted from the back.

"Come here," Leah stated as she sat in the rocking chair waiting for her pregnant friend. "Hell no," NuNu shot back. Leah was crazy to think that she would get up from her bed. "I'm comfortable and I'm not getting up."

Leah couldn't do anything but laugh as she got up and made her way to NuNu's bedroom. Before she climbed in the bed she paused, "y'all haven't been fucking on these sheets have y'all?" she asked knowing they more than likely had.

"Every damn night," Tyson called from the bathroom.

NuNu put her hands over her face shaking her head at his damn mouth. *This boy just says whatever.* Leah had tears falling from laughing so hard.

"Tyson shut the hell up," NuNu finally said, removing her hands from her face.

"What? Leah knows I be making you put a leg by your ear while I'm in that."

"Ty, spare me the details," Leah replied as she took a seat on top of the covers.

"Girl what are you going to do with him," Leah said looking at her friend. Leah made herself comfortable and took the remote from NuNu to find something on T.V. to watch. NuNu was busy reading baby books, so the T.V. was watching her.

"She not going to do nothing with me but love and fuck me good, ain't that right baby?" Tyson stated as he kissed NuNu's lips and rubbed her stomach.

As much as NuNu wanted to talk shit, she didn't. There was no need in telling him to watch his mouth. He was just as blunt as she was but worse. They were just alike so telling him to stop was like telling herself to stop and that wasn't happening.

"That's right baby." She said smirking.

Leah couldn't contain her smile as she looked at the couple in awe. They were beautiful together. Their chemistry was everything. Leah loved the way Tyson loved her friend. NuNu deserved it after what she had gone through with Dominic and Mandy. *Mandy.* Just the very thought of her sent a chill down Leah's spine. She quickly shook the thought from her mind.

"Y'all so cute," Leah complimented after Tyson was done rubbing and kissing his unborn baby.

"Aight baby girl I'm about to bounce, you need anything before I leave?" he asked.

"No, we good," NuNu said, referring to her and the baby.

"Aight, I'll see you later call me if you need anything."

"Okay Ty," NuNu said, getting annoyed because it was the same routine before he left the house for the day. He always wanted to make sure she was comfortable and had everything she needed before he ripped the streets up. He couldn't help it though. She was his first love. His first baby was coming, so he had to make sure they were okay. Tyson made his exit and the two girls began chatting about everything that had been going on lately.

"I finally listened to Mandy voicemail this morning," NuNu announced.

"Did you really?" Leah asked in shock.

She just knew that NuNu would never listen to it. She was certain that her friend had deleted the voicemail a while ago. What Leah didn't know was that NuNu had always had the urge to listen to the voicemail since she received the news about Mandy's death. Regardless of what had happened, NuNu couldn't help but still consider her a friend. NuNu was stubborn but she couldn't just ignore four years of friendship. She wished that she could rewind time and go back to the last day that her and Mandy had faced off. She would have certainly handled it a lot differently, by listening to her friend.

"Yeah," NuNu said sighing as she rubbed her stomach. The baby was stretching her, she rubbed her belly gently smiling at the metamorphosis. It was her way of soothing her love. NuNu felt like every time she touched her stomach it was her way of bonding with her baby.

"I'm actually sorry for how I handled things with her and because of that I forgive her," she said.

136

"That's good Nu, I'm glad," Leah said as her mind drifted back to the dreadful day of Mandy's death. Flashbacks ran through Leah's mind of Mandy kicking the radio and then seeing her body shaking uncontrollably. She then thought about the letter that she had read for Dominic that saved her life from ever having Mandy's death investigated.

"You know she left Nic a letter and I ended up reading it to him Nu, that letter rocked my heart. I didn't know she was battling things with her mother like that."

Leah was now crying.

"I actually can relate to how she feels about her mom because I feel the same way about mine. She came by my g mommy house looking for me and I'm glad I wasn't there," she said, sniffing and wiping at her face.

"Aww boo please don't cry or you are going to make me cry and I do enough of that shit being pregnant," NuNu said looking at Leah with sympathy, trying to keep her tears at bay.

Leah started feeling a churning in her stomach and her mouth salivating. She rushed to the bathroom making it just in time as clear fluids came spewing from her mouth. She was throwing up so hard she got petechiae on her face and started sweating.

"Oh my god," she said to herself after she was finished as she went over to sink to rinse her mouth out with water and then mouthwash that she found in the medicine cabinet above the sink. Leah turned to see NuNu standing in the doorway of the bathroom and she jumped.

"Dammit Nu, why the hell you scare me like that," she said holding her chest.

"Leah Bre'Ana you pregnant, aren't you?" NuNu asked as she shook her head not even wanting her thoughts to be true. She did not want her friend to have a baby with a two-timing nigga like Marcus. He was no good for her and as of lately she couldn't stand even the sight of him, that's why she always remained in her room when he was around.

"I don't think so," Leah said, not wanting to believe it could be true.

Leah wanted no parts of Marcus. He had hurt her to her core with the disrespect. She missed him terribly, but she couldn't see herself giving into what he requested just to have him. A baby would certainly complicate things.

"Leah you've been sick a lot lately. I think you should find out if you're pregnant or not that way you can see what else could possibly be wrong," NuNu said as she turned on her heels and made her way back to her bedroom.

Leah stood there in the middle of the bathroom shaking her head in disbelief. *This can't be happening,* she thought as she tried to remember when her last period was. Her mind raced. She couldn't remember when her last cycle occurred. Leah normally was good with keeping track and she couldn't believe the realization as it smacked her in the face.

"Oh FUUCKK."

Leah ran to NuNu's bedroom.

"I'm fucking late," she yelled as she entered the room.

"I'm fucking late."

NuNu's eyes grew wide and she placed a hand over her mouth and one to her heart. She knew it. She knew that Leah's symptoms were signs of pregnancy. She had

138

experienced the same things when she first found out she was with child.

"Leah. No," NuNu said as she climbed back up from the bed to hug her friend.

"Nu, what will I do if I'm pregnant? I'm scared and I don't want to have a baby with a man like him," Leah said as she cried on her friend's shoulder.

Leah wasn't ready for a baby. Hell, she didn't even want a baby... especially with Marcus. Having a baby was supposed to be special. However, what she and Marcus had going on wasn't special. She didn't want to deal with the attachments that came with him. Leah wanted to finish school without a baby on her hip. She knew a lot of girls in her school walking around with growing bellies. Leah had vowed she would never be one.

"Wait, what happened to you taking your birth control pills?" NuNu asked.

Leah's mind had not been in the right places since the day she ran out of Mandy's house. She had been so wrapped up in trying to take her mind of that day she drowned herself in Marcus and completely forgot to refill her prescription.

"I must have forgotten to refill my script," Leah said, shaking her head and then burying her face in her hands.

"Listen we will go get a test, have you take it and then go from there. You have been stressed out lately with everything that's been going on so maybe it's throwing your cycle off," NuNu said, trying to be positive.

NuNu knew deep down inside that Leah was pregnant. She just hoped like hell that she could be wrong.

"Nu, I'm sure I won't be that lucky just to be stressed out and be late. I bet any amount of money that this boy done trapped me," Leah said as she buried her face back in her hands. *Ain't this about a bitch*, she thought. Leah climbed in the bed, stretching out across the cover. She laid on her side, tucking her hands in between her legs as she cried herself to sleep.

*N*uNu, sat up in bed, head against the headboard rubbing her stomach watching 106 & Park on BET as she waited for Leah to wake up. Leah had been sleeping for the past four hours, sleeping so hard that she never heard when NuNu called Tyson to take her to the pharmacy to get a pregnancy test. NuNu was anxious to know if Leah was pregnant, she wanted to wake her up to pee on the stick. However, she decided to let her sleep and wait for her to wake up on her own. Usher's *You Got It Bad* came on and NuNu couldn't help but to turn it up because it was her song, she loved her some *Usher*. Hearing the video caused Leah to wake up. Blinking her eyes slowly as she rubbed them, she sat up in bed leaning her head on NuNu's shoulder.

"It's a test on the dresser, go pee on it now," NuNu said with authority.

Leah's eyes pierced hers. NuNu was on it. She didn't waste any time now that Leah was up. She had to know.

"Bitch where the hell you get a test from?" Leah asked as her eyes landed on the box sitting on the dresser.

"Girl, just get yo ass up and go pee on it cause I need to know and so the hell do you, GO!"

Leah got up from the bed, rolling her eyes as she walked over to the dresser to get the box. She snatched the box off the dresser, read the back of it and then turned to face NuNu.

"Let's just get one thing straight heffa, you run Tyson and that baby in your stomach, NOT me."

"Girl just go pee on the fucking stick," NuNu said dismissively.

Leah went to the bathroom opening the box along the way. She was so nervous that she was shaking as she sat on the toilet. She began urinating on the stick. *I've ruined my life*, she thought as she finished. Leah placed the stick on the box, while she finished her business on the toilet. She got up and washed her hands and dried them. Leah looked down at the stick and saw two lines appear. Her hands instantly went to her mouth, she was flabbergasted. She looked in the mirror and Mandy's image appeared. Her eyes were boring into Leah's. Leah snapped her eyes shut and then she heard a voice.

"YOU TOOK MY BABY."

Leah stumbled back and fell to the floor. She put her hands to her ears and screamed.

"Nooooo."

NuNu heard the scream and barged into the bathroom. She noticed Leah on the floor and headed straight to her.

"Leah, what's wrong?" NuNu asked.

Leah quickly shook off the paranoia. She couldn't tell NuNu the whole truth, so she opted for telling her part of it.

"Nu, I'm pregnant. What am I going to do? What am I going to do?" Leah wailed.

NuNu squatted down, not wanting to get on the floor because she knew she wouldn't be able to get back up. She rubbed the back of Leah's back as she tried to soothe her.

"Shhh, it's okay boo, remember what you told me, I got you and you got this."

Leah nodded. She closed her eyes and sighed. Only if NuNu knew it was more things that scared Leah than the fact of knowing that she was pregnant.

CHAPTER TWELVE

⬜

$\mathcal{L}$eah called to schedule a doctor's appointment the morning after taking the pregnancy test. The appointment was set for two weeks out, on November 12th. She also had taken a week to process the realization of her being pregnant before she called and told Marcus the news and gave him the date of the first appointment. When the day arrived for the appointment Leah and Marcus sat in the doctor's office, on opposite sides of the room. NuNu and Tyson had dropped her off since she refused to ride with Marcus. He had called that morning asking if she wanted him to come to get her, she had refused. There was nothing to talk about if they were not discussing something regarding the baby.

Sitting in the waiting room, Leah couldn't believe what was becoming of her life. She was only months away from being 19 and was now pregnant. Leah blamed Marcus for her being in this situation. *A baby, what am I going to do with a baby?* she thought. Leah had beat herself up about not being careful and allowing the one thing to happened that she had promised herself and her godmother that she would avoid for as long as possible. She wanted to make something of her life and not be one of those girls that stayed in the projects, living off the government while making babies for the rest of her life.

"Leah Williams," a medical assistant called from the window.

Leah stood headed in her direction with Marcus on her heels.

"Yes, I'm Leah Williams," she said as she approached the counter.

"You can head to the back now, Room A on the left-hand side," the assistant directed.

Walking down the hall Leah's heart was racing, she was getting ready to see how far along she was and possibly hear her baby's heartbeat for the first time. Just the thought of hearing the little human she created heartbeat made her heart swell and eyes fill with tears. They approached the room and went to their designated spot. Leah took a seat on the exam table and Marcus took a seat in the chair right across from her.

"So, we're only going to talk about the baby and that's it?" He quizzed.

"Yep, it is nothing else to discuss," she shot back.

Marcus went to reply but was interrupted by a knock at the door and then a doctor entering.

"Hello, Leah is it?" The doctor asked as he shook her hand.

"Yes," she responded.

"I'm Dr. Asad," he said and then turned to Marcus shaking his hand as well.

"You're the child's father, I'm assuming?"

Marcus nodded and then took a seat. The doctor turned back toward Leah and asked her a few questions before instructing her to remove only her top half of clothing and put on a gown.

"I'll give you 5 minutes and then I'll be back in with my assistant to check on the little one in there."

"You can exit the room as well," she turned to Marcus and said as she snatched the gown from the table.

"Leah you got me fucked up, just hurry up and fucking change before the doctor comes back in here."

Leah rolled her eyes as she lifted her shirt and slid the gown on. She told Marcus to stop staring and he smirked.

"Bey shut up I done seen them little B cups a million times ain't shit changed."

Leah grinned. She found humor in his statement and it lightened her mood a little.

"Don't be calling my chest little, they weren't little B cups when they were all in yo mouth and I'm not your bey, not anymore."

"Okay does fun size sound better? And you gone always be bey," he shot back.

Leah laughed as she climbed back on the exam table just as Dr. Asad and his assistant were knocking at the door before making their entrance.

"Leah and Marcus, this is my assistant Nicole," he stated making an introduction. "She will be in the room while we listen to the baby's heartbeat and take measurements of your belly." Both the doctor and assistant washed their hands as they prepared to get started. Leah laid back as the doctor had requested and the assistant rolled the gown up, tucking it slightly so it wouldn't move.

"Leah, I'm going to apply this gel, it's kind of cold so please be prepared," the assistant warned. She squeezed the gel over Leah's stomach causing her to jump from the coldness. "I told you," the assistant chuckled. The doctor rolled the stool over to Leah carrying the Fetal Doppler with him.

"Okay Leah, just a little pressure as I roll the doppler over your lower stomach to find the heartbeat," the doctor said. Marcus made his way next to Leah grasping her by the hand, as they prepared to hear the best sound ever made. Once Dr. Asad found the right spot on Leah's stomach, they heard a wailing sound that was going pretty fast. Leah couldn't control the tears falling at the sound of their creation, it was music to her ears. She looked up and saw Marcus crying as well, instantly making her heart swell. Marcus swiped a hand down his face and then asked the doctor why were the beats so fast. The doctor explained that the further along Leah got the slower the heartbeat would get as the baby continued to grow.

"Now, let's get this ultrasound going so we can see how far along you are." Dr. Asad stated as he cleaned the doppler, waiting for the assistant to roll the ultrasound machine to him. Marcus was full of questions, asking the doctor everything that came to mind.

"Marcus, let the man do his job please!" Leah snapped

"I am letting him do his job, his job is to answer any questions I got," he snapped back. Leah shook her head and apologized for Marcus's energizer bunny mouth. He just kept going. The doctor chuckled and told them that they made a cute couple. Leah and Marcus looked at each other. They weren't a couple anymore, but they wanted to be. Leah missed her man. She wanted him back but she needed him to do right. Her emotions were now all over the place. Marcus missed her too. He needed his family with him. The doctor had just placed something on both of their hearts with the statement and the room went silent as he gave Leah the ultrasound.

"So, it looks like you conceived in August from the numbers I'm getting, which makes you a little over 3 months and your due date is May 26th."

"Can you tell what she's having?" Marcus piped up.

He was excited and couldn't contain his giddiness. He desperately wanted a boy and he had a feeling that they were going to be having one.

Leah just shook her head, *I wish he shut the hell up with all the damn questions*, she thought to herself.

"No, not yet Dad, on her next appointment if the little one cooperates, I'll be able to give you two that news," the doctor replied. "Until then please take your vitamins that I'm writing you a script for and in two weeks I need you to return to get blood work done." Leah nodded as she sat up wiping her stomach with the towel the assistant handed her. "Okie Dokie, I'll let you get dressed and when you're done head to the nurse's station and make two separate appointments to come back and see me."

Leah dressed and headed for the nurse's station. She was all smiles as she rubbed her small belly. In six months, she would be someone's mother and even though she was happy, she was scared to fail.

$\mathcal{M}$arcus had convinced Leah to ride with him so that they could eat and talk. NuNu had been waiting outside just in case Leah didn't want to ride with Marcus. After confirming that she would be okay, NuNu left but not before letting Marcus know that he better not do shit to piss her friend off. Leah laughed at her friend's threat as she climbed inside the car and buckled up.

"You going to DJ for me mama?" Marcus asked.

"I'm not your mama so don't call me that," Leah said as she picked the cd case up from the floor.

"I know but you're my son's mama, so that's what I'm calling you until he gets here."

"How you know it's a boy Marcus, don't be calling my baby no damn boy since we don't know yet," Leah said as she popped in a mix cd.

"It's a boy, I know it and we're naming him MarKest Anthony Hill."

"Well, what if it's a girl?" She quizzed.

"If it's a girl we're naming her Ma'Laysia Bre'Ana Hill." Leah looked at him with shocked eyes.

"You just made that up or have you been had those picked out?"

"The day you told me you were pregnant I thought of them," he said as he pulled out of the parking lot of the doctor's office.

"You lucky I like them," Leah told him as she tried to find a song she wanted to listen to on the cd.

"Where are we going to get food from?" Leah asked as she leaned back in the seat relaxing. Even though it was the end of fall it was a nice day out, so she cracked the window slightly taking in the fresh air as she enjoyed the ride to wherever they were going. Marcus didn't respond right away as he took over trying to find a song since Leah had given up.

"Just enjoy the ride mama."

Leah closed her eyes and placed a hand on her stomach, as they drove to their destination. Leah didn't realize she had dozed off until she felt Marcus nudging her.

"Wake up mama," he called out.

Leah cut her eyes at him as if he had just woken her up from the best 15-minute nap of her life.

"Stop calling me mama, I told your ass that earlier," she snapped as she exited the car. Marcus rounded the car approaching her and grasping her hand.

"I told you that that's your name so shut up before we go eat at nasty ass Taco Bell across the street instead."

After lunch, Marcus drove Leah home. He wanted to talk to her, he didn't get a chance to tell her everything he wanted to say, everything that he needed to say. Leah agreed, surprising him because she had barely spoken when they were out eating. He let her know that he would be back because he had a few things to take care of.

Leah nodded, got out of the car and headed to her house, hoping her god mom was home so she could show her the pictures from the ultrasound. Even though she didn't know the gender the doctor still printed pictures of the baby for her to have and start a baby album.

"G mommy, you home?" Leah called out as she entered the house.

She heard soft moans as she made her way down the hall. Leah shook her head and banged on Stacy's door telling her to get a room. Stacy laughed.

"I'm in it dammit, get you some business while I'm handling mine."

Leah shook her head and slid the pictures under the door. *She sure has been getting it in lately, with her old ass.*

Leah made her way to her room, kicked off her shoes and stretched out across her bed. The food she ate had her full and she really wanted a nap. *I can't believe I am going to be someone's mother*, she thought to herself. The thought scared the hell out of her. *What if I end up being like my mother, what if I don't love him or her enough and they end up not wanting to deal with me later in life?* Her thoughts were literally jumping her as she tried to calm herself down. Leah was beginning to panic thinking about everything that could possibly go wrong once she stepped into the role of motherhood. Her thoughts were exactly why she didn't want to have children. The things she endured as a child frightened her. She didn't want history to repeat itself once she became a mother. Leah didn't even realize she was crying until she felt the tears roll into her ear. She sat up wiping her face.

"Get it together, Leah you're going to be fine," she said to herself.

She pulled her journal out of her nightstand and began to write. Journaling always soothed her. It allowed her to get her thoughts out of her head without judgement. She began writing down all the things she didn't want to do to her child, that her mother had done to her as a kid. Once she wrote DO NOT HAVE A BROKEN FAMILY, something hit her. It was like a light had clicked on and couldn't be cut off. "If I don't want this, I have to at least try to mend my family now," she mumbled as she pulled her phone out to call Marcus. The phone rang and as she waited for him to answer she heard a knock at the front door. *What the hell is his ass doing?* she wondered, tossing the phone on her bed as she headed to answer the door. Bypassing Stacy's room she could still hear them getting it in. She shook her head.

"Yall nasty," Leah shouted.

"Girl yo ass pregnant so what does that make you?" Stacy shot back.

Leah couldn't help but laugh as she continued for the door.

"Who is it?" she called out before reaching to open it.

"Mama, open up please," Marcus called out from the other side of the door.

Leah snatched the door open smiling. She stared at him. *He one fine hard-headed as nigga.*

"Boy stop calling me that shit."

"MAMA, MAMA, put your shoes back on. Let's go," he said laughing

"You just left here literally 15 minutes ago, you back quick."

"I know, I went to holla at Tyson real quick and came straight back for my baby mama."

Leah rolled her eyes and smiled. *Baby mama*, she thought as she turned and headed for her room to slip her shoes back on. Approaching the living room, she heard Marcus say, "I'll slide through later." When she walked in the room he hung up and stuffed his phone in his pocket. Leah's insecurities immediately started surfacing. *This boy.*

"Um, who was that and where do you think you are sliding through to later?" She quizzed.

"Bey, please don't start, that was City." Marcus answered.

He pulled out his phone showing Leah the last call. Feeling stupid Leah smiled.

"You didn't have to do all that, we ain't together and I don't care anyway," she said smirking trying to play off her insecurity.

"Girl miss me with all that shit, you care or yo Brooke Valentine looking ass wouldn't have asked me no questions in the first place."

Leah smirked, rolling her eyes at the comparison.

"Let's bounce," she said as she opened the door and started walking out.

Leah had made it halfway to the car before she realized she didn't hear Marcus walking behind her. She stopped and turned around. He was still standing on the porch staring down at her.

"Why yo black ass just standing there?" She asked.

Marcus closed the door, making sure it was locked before he made his way down to where Leah was standing. He looked at her for a moment. He missed her and wanted her back. Marcus wouldn't let another day pass without her knowing how he felt. The other girls didn't mean shit to him. They weren't Leah. He knew that from the first day he had set eyes on her. Marcus knew she was special, how he had messed things up so badly he couldn't fathom.

"Leah for real though we gotta make this shit work. I want my kids to be in the same house with their mama and daddy," he voiced affectionately.

"Aight, we can do that blacky," she said playfully.

Marcus smiled and then pecked her lips. The pair turned to walk down the walkway to climb in the car.

"I was actually going to tell you that though," Leah said before she got in the car.

"Word?" He said, stopping on his side of the car.

"Yeah, I wrote down all the things I want for my baby."

"OUR BABY," he said, cutting her off.

"Our baby," she corrected with a smirk, "I wrote down everything I want him or her to have and a one family home was one of them."

"Aight, well that's exactly what THEY will get."

Leah looked at Marcus with shocked eyes. He was saying *they*, as if he and Leah were really going to have multiple. Marcus noticed the look on her face and spoke up.

"Don't look like that, cause right after the first one born, I'm getting you pregnant again. Busting all in that," he said as he put his arms up and did the sexual gesture.

Leah's eyes got wide as she hollered in laughter.

"You sound bout damn dumb, but whatever," she said as she climbed in.

Marcus laughed and climbed in as well.

"Can I drive," Leah asked as Marcus started the ignition.

"You sound bout damn dumb," he answered mocking her pulling away from the curb.

CHAPTER THIRTEEN

☐

Three weeks later

*T*hings between Leah and Marcus were going so well.

Leah was still balancing work and school, but she found herself sleeping more when she wasn't in either place. Mandy's face lived behind her lids and she grew frustrated at the thought of being haunted. She and Marcus stayed cuddled up in their little space in his mama's basement when she wasn't busy with work or school. She needed him close to help ease her mind from the visions and sounds that haunted her. He was her shield and she clung to him as much as she could when she felt Mandy's ghost lingering around.

Early mornings on the weekends were chaotic. Marcus's nieces ran around the damn house yelling and fighting. Leah woke up to the noise every weekend and it always put her in a bad mood. Today was no different. She laid there for a while staring at the ceiling, not being able to return back to dreamland. She finally nudged Marcus, waking him out of his sleep.

"We really need to work on getting our own place, because me listening to these bad ass kids on the weekend is not wassup," Leah said as she kissed his cheek.

"Oh, and let's go buy a space heater for this room cause it's cold as hell down here now that the snow has hit," she told him.

"Aight," he said as he sat up and stretched his arms above his head, yawning.

"They are bad, do you hear them up there cussing?" he asked.

Marcus and Leah made their way upstairs. His nieces had lost their young little minds and Leah was about to do some disciplining. Marcus nieces loved Leah like an aunt, when she spoke they listened. Marcus never introduced any of his female companions to his family. It took them by surprise when he brought Leah around. And when she started coming around often, they knew she was there to stay. Leah entered the living room and the girls headed straight for her, wrapping her in a hug.

"Leah," they called out in excitement.

Leah smirked.

"Mmhmm, y'all better watch y'all mouth cussing like y'all grown. Y'all cuss better than I do," Leah said as she picked her favorite niece up.

"Mama put her big butt down before you strain yourself with my baby in you," Marcus told her.

"Auntie, you having a baby? Is that why your stomach not looking flat no more?" the oldest niece piped up.

"Yeah, I'm going to have your little cousin, so you can't be up here being bad and cussing."

"Who having a baby?" Marcus's mother asked as she made her way down the steps, cutting Leah off. Everyone turned to her as she descended the stairs, making her way into the living room. Marcus's mother was pretty but hard times made her look older than what she really was. His mother was in her early forties but looked every bit of fifty. She was still pretty and was just as sharp as they come.

"Leah I know you not having my son's baby," she said as she walked past and popped her granddaughters in the mouth.

"I heard y'all down here cussing, watch ya mouths cause ya not grown," she said, causing both girls to cry before turning her attention back to Leah.

"So, you pregnant?" she asked, eyeing both Leah and her son.

"Yeah I am," Leah replied as she looked at Marcus in confusion.

Her mind was blown. She didn't understand why he wouldn't share the news with his mother. This would be her first grandbaby coming from him. He should be wanting to let the world know that he was about to be a father. He was excited when they were at the doctor's office, full of questions and working Leah's damn nerves. So how could he not share his happiness with his family?

"So, you didn't tell her?" Leah quizzed.

"Naw," he replied as if it wasn't a big deal.

What the hell is up with him, Leah thought. She couldn't comprehend what his problem was.

"Girl, you were better off telling me cause his ass don't tell me shit. Hell, he barely even speaks to me but got the nerve to be making babies in my damn house."

His mother wouldn't admit it, but her feelings were hurt, and she couldn't even look at him anymore. Leah wore shocked eyes as she looked from Marcus to his mother. She never knew there was so much detachment between her man and his mother. If she saw the look of sadness on his mother's face, she knew he saw it as well. Leah started speaking as his mom started leaving the room.

"Why didn't you tell her boy? I'm 4 months already," she chastised.

"Man, listen I'm not with the 21 questions. I just didn't tell her so drop it," he said terminating the conversation.

Leah rolled her eyes as she brushed passed him, making her exit from the living room and back to the basement. Leah climbed back in bed and let her mind wander on why he hadn't told his mother she was pregnant. In deep thought, she realized that she hadn't told her parents either. She had told her god mother, but Stacy left the decision up to Leah to tell her parents. Leah thought of the conversation with Stacy.

Hell, you are grown and about to graduate, so it's not my place to tell them. You can tell your mom and dad when you feel the time is right. Until then don't rush it or even stress about it. I've had you since you were 11 and at least you waited this long unlike some of these other fast tail heffa's. Also, just so you know rather if you tell them or not or if they help or not just know G mommy got you regardless.

Marcus strolled in the bedroom, snapping Leah from her thoughts on her and Stacy's conversation.

"Listen, mama, I'm so-"

"Don't even say it, it's all good. I can't say anything to you about not telling your mom when I haven't even told my own parents." Leah stated.

Marcus climbed in the bed and laid his head in Leah's lap as she sat up. She smiled as she rubbed his wavy head.

158

Marcus was her big baby and she loved him with everything in her.

"I really hope my baby-."

"Our baby mama damn, OUR baby!" He barked cutting her off.

Marcus was sick of her and this *my* baby shit. He would get annoyed every time she said it. Marcus didn't care if she was trying to be funny. He didn't find humor in it, he helped create their child and when she referred to their baby he wanted to be included. Leah grinned. She knew what she was doing when she started to say her baby. She knew it irritated him. Marcus noticed her grinning.

"Leah, that shit ain't funny."

Leah rolled her eyes and she continued,

"I really hope our baby has my skin color," she said with a grin.

"Fa sho me too," he agreed.

"Are you serious?"

"Yeah, I want all my kids to have your skin color and look like you," Marcus replied.

Leah was divine. Marcus needed his children to be divine as well. He knew that with Leah, they would be just that. She was lovely, his good thing and the realization of that made him remorseful for how he treated her.

"Boy, I told you he or she is the only one we're having, so stop saying it as if we will be having multiple."

"Bey for real," he said lifting from her lap and dead panning on her.

"I'm not with having a bunch of kids with different chicks, so you stuck giving me a basketball lineup"

159

Leah sucked her teeth, as she arose from the bed to get her phone off the dresser. It was time for her to check out of the conversation. Marcus had her messed up if he thought she was cranking out a bunch of children. That was always her fear. She wouldn't become that girl. It was bad enough that's how society looked at black women and Leah just couldn't be that girl. She wouldn't. He was trying to tie her down for real. The first one wasn't supposed to happen and now he was talking about adding more. *He got life all twisted if he thinks I'm having a bunch of fucking kids*, Leah thought. Leah was getting ready to call NuNu to come get her, she needed to get out of the house today and as if NuNu sensed her thoughts, she called.

"Hey heffa," Leah said, answering the phone.

"I was just about to call you to come get me out of the house after I got dressed."

The girls set up a time and hung up the phone. Leah gathered the things for her shower and headed for the bathroom. As she undressed in the basement's full bathroom, she thought about them getting their own place again. Leah stepped into the shower and began singing. She knew she only sounded good in the shower because of the hollow space, so while in there she sang her heart out. She didn't even hear Marcus picking the lock and entering.

Did it feel good to you baby baby
Like it felt good to me

She was singing one of her favorite songs by Xscape *Do You Want To* while Marcus came out of his white basketball shorts and boxers. He watched and listened to Leah sing through the glass door of the shower. He started stroking his man at the sight of her round behind and still perky B cup breasts that were on display. Leah's eyes were closed as she lathered her body until she heard the shower door slide open. Jumping slightly, she dropped the soap and sponge and stared at him.

"Don't bend over to pick up that soap mama or I'm sliding this dick all up in you," Marcus said, licking his lips and gawking.

Leah bit into her bottom lip as she stared at his chocolate body. *Gosh, this boy so damn fine*, she thought as she pulled him in the shower and started sucking on his full bottom lip. Marcus groaned as he stepped in the shower, one foot at a time, grabbing a hand full of her ass and kissed her deep and hard. Between Leah's southern lips it was wet and not because of the showers water either. She was dripping in sweet nectar for him. Leah started stroking his man causing Marcus to let out another groan but this time it was much deeper. The grip she had on his dick made him feel as if he was inside some walls, her walls.

"Damn mama," he said as he leaned his head back enjoying the hand job she was giving. Leah lowered to her knees kissing his stomach on the way down until she got to the tip of his boy and slowly started circling it. Leah was licking as if she were licking around an ice cream cone, trying to stop it from dripping everywhere.

"Shit. What you doing bey?" Marcus asked as he rubbed her head trying to pull her up. Leah had never put her mouth on him, she was always the receiver of the oral pleasure but

161

in this moment, she felt like doing some giving. *Might as well, he's my baby's father and now him and this dick will always be mine*, she thought to herself.

"Mmm Mmm I want to baby just let me for a little bit," she moaned while going back down to make sure the nigga's toes curl while she was putting in work.

Leah started sucking and bobbing as if she knew what she was doing but was using her teeth slightly. Marcus stopped her. If she was going to be doing this, he had to be her coach.

"Slow down baby, don't rush it, tuck your lips under your teeth a little and then suck." Doing exactly as she was told, she was able to get a rhythm going, making his toes curl and then crack. *Damn*, is all he could get out his mouth as he pulled her to her feet kissing her before spinning her around and making her hold the wall. He entered her with the deepest stroke he had ever given her.

"Ahh," she called out as he started pounding her from the back.

Leah's wetness had Marcus ready to bust prematurely. He retreated from inside her and started kissing her back as he dipped two fingers inside her. She yelped. He pulled them out and rubbed them together before sticking them in his mouth, tasting her flavor. Leah turned and noticed what he was doing, and her body shuttered. The sight of his pink tongue savoring her juices gave Leah an orgasm. Marcus reinserted his fingers and twisted. Leah moaned out loud as she clenched her pussy muscles down on his fingers, grinding against them. This boy was skilled. He had to have been a porn star in his previous life because this pleasure was something out of this world.

"Dammit baby," she cried out as she started grinding faster.

"Put it back in baby please, I want to feel you," she said reaching between her legs to replace his fingers with his dick that he kept knocking against her ass. Marcus obliged and dug right back into her.

"Fuuck," Marcus groaned.

Marcus had one hand on each cheek as he watched Leah's womanhood swallow him in and spit him out repeatedly. He knew pussy was good but pregnant pussy was hitting immeasurably different. Marcus threw his head back in ecstasy. With each stroke, he felt a tingle erupt through his body. So many *I love you's* were at the tip of his tongue, but his vocabulary was gone. He couldn't control himself while inside of her and before he got the chance to tell her he was about to bust, she had beat him to the finish line.

"I'm coming baby," Leah squealed as her legs started shaking and getting weak.

Marcus's nieces had heard Leah moaning, so they crept downstairs and were listening on the other side of the door as they finished.

"We telling y'all down here being nasty," they both said in unison as they hit the door giggling and ran back upstairs.

Leah laughed as she began to wash herself.

"We most definitely need our own spot," she said, passing him the soap.

"Yeah we do," he replied back

They finished their shower and got dressed. Marcus left out of the house before Leah did and was in such a rush, he forgot to grab his phone. Leah looked over at the dresser

163

noticing it and strolled right over to it and picked it up. Her heart started racing and her hands started shaking as she flipped the phone open.

Chrissy.

This mufucka still be talking to this bitch, she thought to herself as she went through their messages. Leah saw that they haven't done anything since she found out she was pregnant but still, *what the fuck is he still doing texting this trout mouth hoe?* She thought. Her heart was at her feet. Stacy had always told her not to go fishing unless she was ready for what she would possibly catch. Now that Leah had caught it, she wished she could throw it back. This revelation she didn't want. No, him and Chrissy weren't fucking but them still having dealings with one another still hurt the same. Leah wondered what it was about the girl that he couldn't leave alone. She saw voicemails waiting to be listened to and came up with the perfect plot. Leah dialed into his voicemail guessing his code as the year of his first car a 1986 cutlass supreme. She changed the greeting on his voicemail once it gave her the option.

"Hi, you have reached Marcus and if he is not answering that means 1 of 3 things. He's either sleep, getting to OUR money or he piping me down. Leave a message."

Just as she was finishing, she heard the side door swing open in hast. She hurriedly sat the phone back down in its original place and grabbed her own phone to call NuNu. Marcus walked in on her as she was getting ready to place the call and looked as if he knew something was up.

"Who you calling?" He asked as he walked over to the dresser and grabbed up his phone.

164

"I'm calling Nu to see where she's at, she's taking forever to get here." Leah lied. Her heart was beating so fast and hard that she was almost certain it was visible.

"She's outside, she just pulled up with her non-driving ass," Marcus said, shaking his head.

NuNu had pulled up in the driveway acting like she wasn't going to stop when she saw Marcus coming down the driveway. "You can chill on my friend big homie," Leah said laughing while hoping he didn't realize she dialed into his voicemail, cause she sure in the hell didn't have time to delete the call out of his phone.

"She can't drive and I really don't want you in the car with her while you are pregnant with my baby," Marcus stated as he got serious with her.

"Well, she's here now and I'm leaving, you linking up with City anyways and I'm not about to be stuck in the basement all day bored out of my mind."

"Yeah, whatever," he said heading back out the door.

Leah rolled her eyes, thinking to herself on how he had some nerves to be catching an attitude with his cheating ass. *He better be happy that I didn't just slap his black ass.* Leah grabbed up her purse and headed out the side door right behind him without uttering another word.

CHAPTER FOURTEEN

◻

*L*eah and NuNu had been out searching for apartments for the past month. NuNu especially had been on the hunt, since she found out two days after Christmas that she and Tyson would be having a daughter. She wanted to start getting things prepared for their baby girl. Leah smiled as she thought about how her and NuNu's baby would be god siblings. Her mind then drifted to Mandy being pregnant as well and how all three of them would have been having babies around the same time. When the thought hit her, she wondered if NuNu ever responded to the apology Dominic sent to her via text message, she only mentioned listening to Mandy's voicemail. "Hello, earth to Leah," NuNu said, pulling her from her wonders.

"Heffa where you want to get food from before we go back to my house?" NuNu asked. "Huh," Leah said, not hearing her completely.

Thoughts of Mandy had her head in a different place. She wished she could rewind the hands of time and go back to the tragic day. She would have handled the matter another way. *Mandy would be here if it weren't for me,* she thought.

"Where. Do. You. Want. To. Get. Food. From?" NuNu said in a stupid voice and twisting her fingers in crazy ways as she broke down each word.

"Oh, I don't care," Leah shrugged.

The girls arrived at Wendy's, making their way inside the building, trying to hurry out of the snow. They placed their orders and took a seat in the back of the dining area. "Nu did Mandy tell you she was pregnant in her voicemail?" Leah asked as she stuffed a fry in her mouth. NuNu took a bite of her salad as she let the question linger for a moment before answering. "NuAsia I know you heard me," Leah stated, snatching NuNu's fork out of her hand. NuNu snatched the fork right back.

"First of all don't be calling me by my government and second yes she told me Leah." "Why didn't you tell me?" Leah asked.

"Heffa I just heard that part this morning while me and Ty were on our way to the doctors for the baby.

"Wellll, spit it out, what all did she say? I mean you listened to it before, but we never got into details of what was in the message," Leah pushed as she leaned in close. "Leah you can lean your big forehead as back shit," NuNu said, rolling her eyes, she really wasn't in the mood to talk about it.

She was passed what had happened and was moving on from it. She no longer held any hate in her heart for her deceased friend. NuNu understood that sometimes love could make you do things you weren't proud of. Mandy had always craved Dominic, it was what her heart desired. She was simply trying to feed her heart what it was hungry for. Mandy had never felt love, she desperately wanted it from Dominic and as messed up as the situation was, he provided it. He gave her the love that she required. After NuNu realized all of this she was no longer mad, she no longer held

167

resentment. She wished that things could have been handled in a different manner. However, it was done and over with. There was no sense in her crying over spilled milk. She simply cleaned it up and kept it moving.

"Leah let's just drop it," NuNu said dismissively.

Leah surrendered, changing the subject. If NuNu wasn't in the mood she wouldn't dwell on it any longer.

The girls finished their food and headed back to NuNu's house.

"Was Ty happy about the baby being a girl?" Leah quizzed.

"Nope," NuNu said laughing as she turned into the driveway of her home. The way she pulled in scared Leah as she thought about when Marcus said NuNu couldn't drive.

"Damn heffa slow down, you act like it ain't snow on the damn ground," Leah said, holding the dashboard.

"Girl shut up, I know what I'm doing," NuNu shot back.

The girls were about to step out of the car until Leah stopped NuNu as the idea of a middle name popped in her head. They had talked about baby names while they were eating and had come up with Ma'Leah for the first name but couldn't decide on a middle name.

"Girl, I just thought of a middle name," Leah said, grabbing at NuNu's arm.

"What, what is it?"

"Jewel," Leah said smiling.

NuNu smiled and hugged her sister in excitement.

"You are the bomb, how in the hell didn't I think of that? Ma'Leah Jewel Wilson," NuNu repeated with a soft voice. "I love it Leah, thank you." Leah smiled as they both got out of the car and walked up to the house. The middle name sounded just like Tyson's middle name which is JuRell. Leah couldn't believe NuNu didn't think of it, being that it was her man. Once inside Leah kicked off her Timberland boots and came out of her Pelle Pelle coat as she headed straight for NuNu's rocking chair with her bag of food in hand. NuNu took a seat on the long couch and they both dug into their food. They had just eaten and still ordered food to go before leaving the restaurant. You could tell these girls were pregnant the way they were devouring their food as if they had not eaten in years.

*T*yson and Marcus walked into the house from drinking and kicking it on the block. Tyson was instantly pulled towards NuNu once he saw her lying on the couch, one hand tucked between her thighs and the other resting under her face. *She is so damn beautiful.* Tyson smiled, he felt like the luckiest dude in the world right now. He had the prettiest girl he had ever laid eyes on and was about to be a father. He couldn't ask for a feeling that was better than this. The type of passion he had for NuNu was once in a lifetime and he planned to hold onto it. He actually wanted to hold onto her for a couple of lifetimes because she was a rare creation that he knew God had created for him only. Tyson admired her for a moment before lifting her in his arms, causing her to wake up from her food coma. NuNu's appetite had picked up a lot lately and she was always tired.

"Hi Ty," she said, nuzzling her nose in his neck as she threw one arm around him.

"Wassup baby girl, I see you've been eating good," he said with a smirk as he carried her down the hall and into the bedroom. He laid her on the bed and then removed her pants and t-shirt so she could be comfortable. A whiff of alcohol invaded NuNu's nostrils and she recoiled. Tyson wasn't a drinker and the smell of liquor coming from him caught her off guard.

"Ty, have you been drinking?" She asked as she assisted him with the shirt. He nodded as he came out of his clothes and then slid in the bed right next to her.

"I've never known you to be a drinker Ty, what's up?" NuNu asked as she scooted closer to him invading his space. Something was off. NuNu knew her man well, him drinking alarmed her and she needed to make sure he was okay.

"Me being a father is what's up baby girl, what if I don't get this shit right?"

Tyson was nervous about stepping into fatherhood. Him and Marcus had driven around the city indulging in a bottle of Hennessy as he thought of the step he was getting ready to take. He had never had his father around, it was always him and his mother. His uncle had stepped in when he hit his teenage years, but it still didn't make up for him being fatherless. Tyson wanted to get this father thing right the first time around. He didn't want to make mistakes along the way

170

and then know what to do the second time around, because he was definitely having more kids with NuNu.

NuNu sat up in bed and rested her head against the headboard as she motioned for him to lay in her lap. He naturally gravitated to her stomach and laid his head softly against it. "See Ty, you're going to be so good to her. You always just lay your head next to my stomach and whisper things, like you're having your own private little conversation with your child. You're amazing to me and I know for a fact you're going to be amazing to our daughter." NuNu couldn't let him believe that he would fail. He was good to her and she knew whole heartedly that he would be good to their baby. Tyson rubbed her belly softly.

"Hey princess Ma'Leah, I can't wait to see your pretty face," he said softly.

The connection he was making with their baby warmed NuNu's entire heart. She couldn't help but smile as she rubbed the top of his head softly and watched him have a moment with their baby.

"I figured out a middle name for her," NuNu whispered.

"Oh yeah, shoot it," he said.

"Jewel."

Tyson lifted from her belly.

"Who came up with that?" he asked as he kissed her thighs.

"I did," she lied as she moaned softly.

Tyson smirked as he continued to kiss her thighs. He knew she was lying because Leah had already texted him and told him she came up with the name, so she was telling him cause she knew NuNu would take the props and that's exactly what she did. Tyson made his way to her inner thigh and licked her slowly, sending chills through her body. NuNu reached for her breast and started flicking them as she laid there enjoying his soft tongue and rough hands on her, roaming her body. Tyson scooted down the bed and pulled at NuNu's legs gently, causing her to lay down as he slid her panties down all in one motion. Spreading her legs, he messaged her thighs as he trailed his tongue up her right one. He then kissed down the small soft patch of hair on NuNu's treasure box. She preferred it all gone but he loved the small trail she left since it was soft and light. She just figured it was how they liked it on the east coast. Once he got to her split he kissed there and she moaned and the pulse in her pussy intensified. Tyson licked her clit like he licked his spoon after taking a bite of yogurt. That had NuNu's juices flowing as she bit into her bottom lip, loving every moment.

"Tyson baby I love you," NuNu whispered.

She watched him rotate his head in a circle in between her thighs. That nigga spoke very fluent cunnilingus and NuNu loved it when he did. Her stomach tightened. She threw her arm over her face as he went to work. Tyson was in the middle of her construction site putting in hard labor as NuNu sat there admiring the work he was doing.

"Damn lor mama," he groaned.

"You fucking dripping wet for me, you must of been ready to get bizzy."

He began to stroke his man as he licked and sucked on her pussy. He gave her one long firm stroke of his tongue and that was it, NuNu was ready to fuck.

"YES!" She shouted.

Tyson had her squirming, she was so ready.

"Tyson, baby come on," she said softly yet demanding.

That was all she needed to say and he was in her within seconds.

"Oh shiitt, Nu'Asia," he said as he rocked in and out of her at a slow pace.

NuNu instantly started clawing at his back. Tyson thanked God he had on a white beater because he was certain that she would have drawn blood.

All of a sudden they heard a loud thud and Leah screaming.

"What the fuck?" Tyson said as he jumped up and tossed his shorts back on.

BOOM

What the hell? NuNu thought. She hurriedly slid on some shorts and shirt as well. She was right on Tyson heels as they made their way to the living room to see what all the screaming was for. When they entered the room, they saw Marcus hovering over Leah slapping her in the face. That set NuNu on fire as she charged him and punched him in the back of the head.

"Get the fuck off my sister," she yelled as she hit him again this time catching him in the side of his ear.

The punch knocked Marcus to the side as it dazed him a bit. Tyson grabbed NuNu moving her to the side just in case Marcus tried to retaliate.

"Nu, move, get Leah up and y'all go to the backroom." He barked.

Leah was a crying mess and her lip was throbbing. She touched it, wincing as she pulled back bloody fingers. The sight of the blood caused Leah to go crazy. She had never been hit by a boy before and now she was a victim of abuse. She had witnessed her mother being abused and vowed to herself that she would never endure that type of pain.

"Fuck you, Marcus," she screamed as she tried to attack him.

"How the fuck you going to hit me cause I caught you texting a bitch? Fuck you nigga I'm done," she continued to yell as NuNu tried pushing her to the bedroom.

Marcus stood to his feet still slightly stunned from the blow. He was drunk on top of that and could barely stand. The effects of the liquor had him feeling stuck.

"Bro, what the fuck is your problem?" Tyson said, turning to him.

Tyson didn't know how the Toledo niggas got down but back home laying hands on a woman meant you were weak. He didn't believe in a man striking a woman and he wasn't about to allow it under his roof. Leah had become like a little sister to him and there was no way he was going to allow any man to cause her harm. Tyson would rock Marcus's jaw if he ever caught him using her as a punching bag again.

"Nigga why the fuck you putting your hands on my lor sister, we don't do that shit around these parts," he said as he pushed him toward the front door.

"Bro, man I don't know what the fuck I was thinking man, that's not even me I've never put my hands on no bitch before," Marcus stated. He was so intoxicated that he slurred the words. It was clear that Marcus couldn't handle his liquor and Tyson made a mental note that he could never sip with him again. Not when it would cause Leah harm.

174

"Aye, you can chill with calling her a bitch, cause we don't do that shit either my nigga." Tyson stated, swiping his nose as he opened the door. Tyson couldn't believe the amount of disrespect that was coming from Marcus's mouth. He was just in Tyson's car telling him how much he loved Leah and how he wanted to be better for her. Now here he was hitting her and calling her a bitch. His actions were the complete opposite of the words he spoke not even an hour ago.

"Let's go outside and get some fucking air man, you tripping," Tyson said, pushing him out the door.

Before they could even make it all the way out, Leah came running from the backroom. She was pissed and needed to release the aggression that was built up. She tried to swing on Marcus, but Tyson intercepted her, swooping her up and placing her on the couch. Marcus noticed her lip and his eyes widened. *What the fuck did I do?* he thought.

"Leah baby I'm so fucking sorry," he said as he tried to approach her.

"Don't even think about it you black ass Dave Chapelle looking muthafucka, I never did like your ugly ass," NuNu spat as she blocked him and folded her arms across her chest. She was not about to let him get to her, pregnant or not NuNu was ready to fight. She secretly wished that he had pushed her or something from punching him, so Tyson could have beaten his ass.

"All y'all need to chill the fuck out," Tyson yelled.

He had had enough of the bullshit. Tyson turned to NuNu and pointed to her rocking chair, making her take a seat. The look on his face let her know that he was serious, and she did what she knew she was being told. "What the fucking is y'all problem?" Tyson asked, turning and facing Leah. She dropped her head in her hands as she began to cry. Marcus had passed out while in the middle of typing a text, he was that drunk. Leah had grabbed his phone from his hand and felt like she had been slapped. He was in the middle of texting Chrissy. *He just won't leave this bitch alone*, Leah had thought. Leah had tried to refrain from crying but the magnitude of the situation was so overwhelming, the tears just fell effortlessly. She had tossed the phone back at him causing him to wake up and the fight started from there.

NuNu watched her friend in turmoil and spoke up. "Leah fuck this nigga, you don't need this muthafucka. All he do is fucking cheat and now this, putting his hands on you like you not pregnant and like you're not a fucking woman, FUCK HIM!" She spat venomously.

Marcus had got on NuNu's bad side and once you were on it you stayed there. She surely could careless about the nigga being drunk, because that wasn't an excuse for him to be putting his hands on the mother of his child. Hell, there would never be an excuse to lay hands on a woman for any reason. He was weak. A coward and she wanted to hit his ass again for the disrespect.

"Aye, baby chill, I don't need you worked up and stressed out." Tyson cut in.

"Naw, fuck that, he shouldn't have hit my fucking sister." She said.

NuNu looked over and saw Leah lip swelling and went to the kitchen to get her some ice.

I can't stand this bitch, she always got some shit to say. I should have smacked her ass too, Marcus thought to himself as he eyed NuNu walking into the kitchen.

NuNu came back to the living room with the ice pack for Leah. She held it to her friend's lip and then looked at Tyson.

"Tyson if you ever fucking think about cheating and putting your hands on me nigga you gone find yourself in an early grave, don't let this nigga influence you," NuNu warned him.

NuNu kept going on and on about how he bet not do this or he bet not do that or else. She talked mad shit as she soothed Leah, who was laying on her shoulder crying.

"Nu'Asia, yo shut the fuck up with that shit ma. You bumping them gums for no reason. I'm my own man can't no nigga influence me to do shit." Tyson barked as he approached her. He invaded her space, getting right in her face. He needed her to hear him good. NuNu looked at him in shock, he had never spoken to her with the tone he was using. "You talking all this shit when I really just need you to talk some nasty shit in my ear while I'm hitting that cause I'm about to finish getting my nut off. All three of y'all got me fucked up with all this dumb shit," he barked leaning back up and eyeing all of them. The entire room just stared at him. He was pissed and it showed. Tyson was always the calm, laid back one but tonight they got a different version of him. "Come on dummy let me get you home," he said to Marcus. He wasn't with the drama and was ready for everyone to leave. He still had unfinished business to attend to.

"Nu, take Leah home and when I get back you better be in that bed naked and ready for me with wet pussy cause I'm coming back to lay this pipe." He stated with authority.

NuNu's face turned warm and a pulse had started instantly in between her thighs. Tyson's mouth always turned her on. This version she was getting of him tonight had her feeling like they were role playing and he was being a bad boy for her. She couldn't wait for him to get back home because the way he had her soaking for him, she needed him to dry it up with that mannish mouth.

"Nu just run me home cause Ty sounds like he is not playing with you," Leah said laughing and then wincing from the pain in her lip. NuNu smirked and then twirled her fingers in her curls as she glanced at Tyson. *Him and that fucking mouth,* she thought. NuNu pulled her bottom lip into her mouth, trapping it in between her teeth and then slowly released it.

"Let me throw on some different clothes and I'll run you home," she said. NuNu headed to her room while the boys made   their   exit.

178

CHAPTER FIFTEEN

☐

*N*uNu dropped Leah off and raced home to set a scene up for Tyson. She heard his music as he was pulling up 5 minutes after she walked in the door. NuNu hurriedly undressed, lit a few Glade candles and started some slow music. She was laying in the bed naked with wet pussy like he ordered when he walked in.

"Welcome back big daddy," she said.

NuNu climbed up on her knees, pinching her right nipple and massaged her wetness.

"Big daddy huh," Tyson said as he bricked from the sight of her and started coming out of his clothes. NuNu nodded.

"I see you listened to big daddy and was in this bed naked," he said biting into his bottom lip with those perfect white teeth.

He stood there for a moment taking her in and loving the scene that was playing out in front of him. NuNu was beautiful while pregnant. Her weight was going to all the right places and Tyson loved every bit of it. She looked at him with seductive eyes and beckoned for him to approach her with one finger. Tyson looked around the room giving a little foreplay and pointed to himself. NuNu nodded and laid back on the bed as he approached. He climbed in the bed slowly kissing her up her thighs. Tyson stopped at her center and kissed her there. One quick peck was all that was needed. "I fucking love you Nu'Asia," he said sliding into her flowing river. NuNu gasped as he filled her. He was so thick and hard that she felt like he was stretching her walls beyond its limits.

"I love you too Ty, so much."

Tyson lifted one leg as he stroked her and licked up and down her leg slowly.

"Fuck baby, you so damn wet," he moaned.

NuNu moaned as she worked her hips to his rhythm. Donell Jones *Natural Thang* was crooning from the speakers and was perfect for the mood. Tyson took his time with NuNu as he explored her depths.

"Damn baby you feel so good right now," he groaned as he let her leg down and carefully laid on top of her, never stopping his stroke. When he got close enough NuNu went crazy in his ear.

"You wanted me to talk that nasty shit right daddy?" She whispered as she licked his ear slowly.

"Mmhmm," he grunted.

"Well go crazy in this pussy baby, pipe me down from talking shit tonight."

Tyson moaned as he grew even harder. He was so hard that it both felt good and hurt. When he stiffened, it caused NuNu to gasp. Tyson started going beast on her as he quickened his pace, rocking her love box because this feeling of pleasure was something different for the both of them. Tyson normally made love to her always gentle but tonight he was giving her a combination of both love making and fucking.

"Shit," NuNu cried out.

Tyson lifted swiftly pulling NuNu up with him and turning her around, not too rough but just right as he entered her from the back. He was giving it to her inch by inch and she took it all. The way they were fucking you would have thought she wasn't pregnant already. They were going at it as if they were truly trying to go half on a baby. Their sex tonight was so raw and passionate, sexing like they had points to prove.

"Ahhh," she whimpered as he pounded her from the back.

"You wanted to be piped down right?" He asked as she slapped her ass and then rubbed it soothingly.

"Yes daddy," she cried as she lowered her body to the bed.

Tyson lifted her back up and made her arch that back. She wanted to be piped down, so she was going to take every stroke he gave her. He gave her a deep thrust causing her to yelp.

"Naw, baby girl get that ass back up and take this shit." He ordered.

"Tyyyy," she cried out as she bit into the sheets. As if she got a burst of energy and ounce of courage, she threw it back at him, catching Tyson off guard and shocking herself.

"Damn," he said looking down at her. *Where the fuck did that just come from.* Tyson grinned as he enjoyed the sight. NuNu never performed so well and tonight she was going to be receiving a standing ovation. A round of applause was in fucking order because this, this was her best work. Tyson couldn't have been more proud. He lifted his head toward the ceiling and put both hands on top of his wavy head as he let her work.

"You better throw that shit," Tyson coached. She caught the beat of the music playing and threw it back to that beat. She was working him good cause he was groaning like never before. She felt him stiffen like she knew he was about to explode and turned around and went to put her mouth on him, but Tyson stopped her. "No baby lay down we're going to finish this shit together," he said as he slid back into her from the front. The sound of NuNu moaning and calling his name drove Tyson crazy. His head was spinning from the intense pleasure. Tingles went through his body as she caressed his back. "I'm about to bust baby," Tyson told her as he kissed her neck and began to pump faster. The second NuNu felt his manhood expand in her sent a wave of sparks throughout her entire body.

"Agh," she cried out as she joined him in ecstasy.

You took my baby from me. Leah's eyes popped open as she sat up scrambling against the back of her headboard. Another nightmare. Leah had another nightmare about Mandy saying she took her baby. She had these dreams often since finding out she was with child. Leah held her covers to her chest as she cried. Her life was getting out of hand. The things she was battling within herself was torcher. The fighting with Marcus was hell. She took a deep breath and wiped her face. *I have to tell someone*, she thought. Leah got up from the bed slowly, body aching from her and Marcus fighting the previous night. She went to lick her lips but winced remembering her lip was busted and swollen. *This nigga really put his hands on me*, she thought to herself, walking to the bathroom to brush her teeth and wash her face.

Leah looked in the mirror and tears started falling. Her life right now was not what she had planned. She had been abused and she didn't know how to feel. Her emotions were everywhere. She cried for about 5 minutes before getting herself together and doing what she went in there to do. Once she finished, Leah went to the kitchen and took a seat at the table.

"Morning g mommy," she said as she poured orange juice into the cups that Stacy had sitting on the table for them both.

"So, you want to tell me why in the hell *YOU* didn't tell me that Marcus put his fucking hands on you Leah Bre'Ana."

When Stacy used both names Leah knew not to play with her. Her godmother wanted the truth and not one detail was to be left out. Leah lowered her head.

"You were sleeping mommy and I didn't want to wake you up."

"Leah don't play with me, I don't care if I was in the middle of fucking or sucking dick, you tell me what the hell is going on at all times. That boy has left you with a swollen lip and a bruise on your damn face." Stacy was so pissed she had burnt the last batch of sausage she was making. She turned the stove off and went back to the table with Leah.

"Now what the hell happened cause NuNu could only tell me some of it before Ty made her get off the phone."

"When did you talk to her?" Leah asked.

"It doesn't even matter, just tell me what the fuck happened," Stacy said as she folded her arms across her chest and waited for Leah to tell the story.

Leah went on to tell her what happened not leaving anything out. Stacy listened, never interrupting as she grew angry. She raised Leah to be better and the fact that she was allowing a boy to disrespect her set her on fire. Stacy had poured her heart out to Leah about what to accept and what not to accept in a man. She shared a few of her own experiences, hoping that Leah would take them as a lesson.

"Leah, listen I know that is your child's father and you love him but don't ever let no nigga disrespect you and strip you of your worth. I know, baby girl I get it you want to have a stable family but that nigga putting his hands on you and especially while you pregnant is not okay."

"I know mommy," Leah said as she lowered her head.

"Lift your head baby girl and listen," Stacy said.

She grabbed Leah by the chin and tilted her head back up. She wanted Leah to look her in the eye like a woman and embrace what she was saying. Leah wasn't her little girl anymore, so Stacy was going to spit game to her like that grown woman Leah was trying to be.

"You deserve better than what this nigga putting you through. It seems like ever since school started back up he's been on some other shit with you and now that you are pregnant he's really on one like he owns you now. Don't give him any power over life Leah, baby father to be or not. You be your own woman and don't let no nigga take ownership of you EVER."

"Yes ma'am," Leah replied.

"So what do you plan to do about y'all situation Leah?" Stacy asked.

Leah had no words. She just sat there staring as her mind raced. She didn't have a clue what she wanted to do. She loved him and wanted to make it work. Leah wanted nothing more than to have a family. *Gosh, I really don't want to let this go, but is it really worth all this bullshit?*

Stacy took Leah's silence for an answer.

"You do what's best for you baby girl but remember what I said."

Leah nodded and headed to her room.

"Oh, and he not allowed in my house no more. If I see him, I'm going to cut his ass for putting his fucking hands on my baby and grandbaby," Stacy called out.

Leah entered her room and laid across her bed in deep thought. She cried into her pillow as she thought of all the things she was going through. *I just had to stop for this nigga when we first met,* she pondered. Stacy knocked at the door disrupting Leah's thoughts.

"Marcus punk ass is outside. Leah, I'm telling you now if this nigga knocks on my door, I'm going to blow his fucking head off."

Stacy's tone was laced with malice. She shut Leah's door and went back to the kitchen. Leah sat up and wiped her eyes. She got out of the bed, slid her Reeboks on and ran to

185

the door. Leah opened the door just as Marcus made his way on the porch.

"No, go back to the car now," Leah said, looking back toward the kitchen as she closed the door. He looked at her in confusion as she pushed him back down the steps and followed behind him. "My G mommy knows what happened and she's hot right now," Leah warned as they got in the car. Marcus went on about how he was sorry and that it would never happen again. He apologized only about putting hands on her. He never acknowledged the situation with Chrissy. Leah had enough with the excuses and was ready to end the conversation. Since he didn't address everything, Leah was ready to get out of the car. She shook her head.

"No, Marcus I don't want to hear your sorry's. I don't want to hear it anymore because you just keep doing shit that you have to be sorry for."

"LEAH!" Stacy yelled from the porch with her Beretta in hand. Leah must have thought her godmother was playing. She had to think she was playing or thought she was talking just to hear herself talk. Whatever Leah was thinking she knew better. She knew Stacy well enough to know that she said what she meant and meant what she said. Stacy always walked what she talked.

"Shit," Leah said as she opened the car door making her way out of the car.

"What?" Marcus said, wondering what was going on.

"I think you should just leave," Leah said as she looked back up toward the porch.

She knew Stacy wouldn't hesitate to use her gun. Stacy's father was country and they stayed shooting out in open fields just for fun. However, this situation wasn't for fun. Marcus had violated her baby and she was trying everything in her to keep restraints since he was Leah's baby's father. That earned him a pass. Barely.

"I'll be back mama." He yelled.

"No the fuck you won't," Stacy yelled back.

She let off a shot toward the tree right next to his car. Leah ducked and Marcus pulled off recklessly from the curb. "Leah get your ass in the fucking house cause you're not going no damn where." Leah stood to her feet and walked into the house and didn't mumble a word. Retreating to her bedroom Leah turned on her radio and laid across her bed. *My g mommy is freaking crazy*, she thought. She pulled out her phone and sent NuNu a text.

Leah: Girl my mama just shot at Marcus

My Nu: Good. Fuck that black ass bitch with his ugly ass

Leah couldn't reply fast enough. Another text came across her screen.

My Nu: Did she hit him?

Leah laughed she knew NuNu couldn't stand Marcus with a passion and would be happy to hear about what just happened.

Leah: No, Nu she didn't damn.

My Nu: that makes me sad...

Stacy opened Leah's door without giving her the courtesy of knocking because she was pissed. Leah sat up and turned the radio down as Stacy stood in the door.

"You care to tell me why you are constantly having nightmares about Mandy?"

Leah grew nervous. She didn't expect that question and had she been standing it would have surely knocked her off her feet.

"Where did that just come from?" Leah replied.

"Just answer the damn question. This is the fourth time I heard you say you're sorry to her in your sleep, but this Marcus situation made me remember to ask since you were saying it when I came in here this morning." Stacy said.

She had never seen Leah so disturbed. She noticed a change in Leah ever since Mandy's death. Stacy had thought it was Marcus being a distraction, but something was telling her that it was more to it.

"I don't know mommy. I guess I feel guilty for jumping her and then finding out she was pregnant after she passed." Leah whispered, telling half the truth. She couldn't imagine telling her godmother the truth about what really happened to Mandy that day and that she was the cause of her death. Leah wanted to tell her, but she couldn't. The words sat at the tip of her tongue, but she couldn't let the words flow. *She did say I can tell her anything*, Leah thought. She wondered how Stacy would react if she exposed the truth. *I have to tell her, maybe she could help me sort through this mess*, Leah coached herself. She started building up the nerve and courage to tell her dark secret.

"Mommy," Leah called out. Her voice barely audible.

"Don't mommy me, Leah what is it?" Stacy said, staring at her with piercing eyes.

Leah took a deep breath and then exhaled.

"I have something to tell you."

"I said what is it, Leah?" Stacy said in frustration.

She was already pissed about Marcus and now Leah was sitting here stalling instead of speaking her mind like she had always taught her.

"Nothing, never mind," Leah said.

She dropped her head and could no longer will herself to finish the truth. She decided to keep it to herself. Leah didn't think she could ever reveal the truth of why she was having nightmares, to anyone. Stacy looked at her and sucked her teeth. She wasn't about to play stupid games with her right now.

"Bre'Ana don't you fucking leave this house if that punk ass boy decides to come back over here and I'm not playing," she said exiting without another word.

Leah's phone rang and she looked at it to see Marcus calling. She let it ring and allowed it to go to voicemail. Moments later her phone rang again and this time she answered.

"Hello," Leah said.

"Leah come outside, I'm down the block," Marcus responded.

"No, Marcus I'm done with you, go be with your hood rat since you can't seem to leave her alone." Leah shot back

Leah listened to the apologies that Marcus was pouring out. He blamed his actions on being drunk. Leah didn't care. He was still refusing to speak on Chrissy and why they were still communicating. Marcus began to cry over the phone. Hearing his cries made Leah let her guard down. She had never heard him so broken and it touched her. *He's sorry.*

"Are you crying?" Leah asked.

"Naw man," Marcus said, trying to sniff away his emotions.

"Yeah you are, I'm coming out."

She hung up the phone and threw on her black and white *Baby Phat* velour sweat suit. Leah quickly pulled her hair into a ponytail and then placed a cap over her head. She slid on some Reeboks and crept out of her room. She heard the shower going and dashed for the front door. She made her way up the street to where she saw Marcus had his car parked and got in without looking or speaking to him. He drove them to his house and they made their way to their secluded spot in the house. Marcus entered his bedroom first and Leah halted at the door. She scanned the room, *what the hell am I even doing here*? She thought.

"Please Leah come here," Marcus pleaded.

She stepped inside, kicking his pants out the way. Her heart sank at what she saw lying on the floor. Her mouth fell open and her eyes prickled. Time seem to have frozen as she eyed the item on the floor. She looked up to him and then back to the floor. Leah couldn't speak and knot had formed in her throat. Her mind was screaming for her to release her emotions. It was telling her to release the thoughts before they exploded in her head. She tried her best not to let the tears fall that was clinging to her eyelashes. Leah felt the first tear fall and then the rest fell effortlessly as she finally let her emotions break free.

"Are you fucking serious?" she shouted as she turned to leave.

Marcus looked down and saw the used condom laying on the floor. "Fuck," he said under his breath as he chased after her. He had fucked up again.

"Leah baby wait."

Leah spun around on her heels so fast and socked him dead in the face.

"Fuck you," she spat and then took off running up the stairs. Marcus shook off the blow and caught her before she made it to the door, grabbing her from behind. He wasn't about to be chasing her all over the place. He yanked her by the arm forcefully as he pulled her down the stairs. "No!" She yelled and attempted to get back to the door. This time Marcus smacked her, and she fell into the wall dazed. Leah leaned against the wall with her hand to her face. He pulled her up and forced her down the stairs. She cried the entire time as he marched her to his room and forced her on the bed.

"I bet yo ass don't hit me again," he said as he watched her hold her face while sobbing into the pillow. Leah didn't respond. She just laid there, one hand holding her face and the other hand on her stomach. Marcus climbed onto the bed and put his hand on top of hers. Instant guilt hit him as he rubbed her stomach.

"I'm sorry mama," Marcus said with a whisper. Leah continued to ignore him as she laid there crying, thinking how he was crazy. How he could go from abusive to I'm sorry with a snap of finger, scared her. Marcus continued to talk to her while he rubbed her stomach. He was begging and pleading. His sorry fell on deaf ears because Leah had tuned him out. She felt that it was God punishing her for what she did to Mandy. She was only 18 and enduring things that she should never be experiencing. She was supposed to be going to games with her friends and enjoying her senior year in high school. Life had become hard and she believed it was her karma.

"I'm sorry and this shit won't happen again I promise you," Marcus said with sympathy.

"Something is wrong with you, I can't stay with you Marcus," she said sniffing as she tried to move his hand.

Marcus forced his hand back to her stomach rubbing and still pleading. He climbed off the bed while making Leah sit up and face him. He kneeled in front of her as he held her arms and stared at her. She could barely look at him, instead of staring back she looked off to the side. Tears slid down her face freely. He turned her face back towards him.

"Leah please give me one more chance, I promise to never do this shit again."

"Who was she?" Leah finally asked, ignoring his plea.

Marcus dropped his head. To let it be known that it was Chrissy that he was still messing with would hurt Leah. He knew that for sure.

"Who was she, Marcus?" Leah asked again this time with tears falling.

Leah knew it was Chrissy, she just knew. He couldn't seem to leave the girl alone. Their fights and arguments always revolved around her. Leah started to wonder if he was torn between the two. Chrissy had been around just as long as she had, and Leah felt like she was in competition with the girl. Knowing it was her, Leah still wanted to hear it from his mouth. She was hoping that maybe, just maybe she was wrong. She honestly preferred for it to be a new bitch than for it to be Chrissy's dirty ass.

"If I tell you," he paused for a minute. Marcus didn't want to go further with admitting the truth. He knew that Leah would probably get up and try to leave again if he exposed it.

"If you what?" she said.

"Leah you won't stay if I tell you, I know you won't."

"I'm not going to stay if you don't tell me the truth, now who was she?" Leah shot back.

"It was Chrissy," he replied in a low tone.

Even though she knew all along, just hearing it caused her to double over as she cried. The realization that it was Chrissy gutted Leah. Her chest tightened as if someone was squeezing her on the inside.

"You just can't leave that bitch alone can you?" She asked.

"Yeah, I can. She doesn't mean shit to me. She kept pitching that shit at me and last night I caught it. I was drunk Leah and when I got home after leaving Nu house I was horny as fuck and wasn't going to bed with a hard dick."

Leah gave him a look of disgust. Marcus was a dawg. Leah now understood why NuNu couldn't stand him. Shit, she was getting to a point where she couldn't stand him either. Leah's emotions were all over the place. This pregnancy had her both loving and hating him, all at the same time. Why couldn't he get this right? It was supposed to be just as simple as the song she used to sing when she was little. That *first comes love, then comes marriage, and then*

193

comes a baby in a baby carriage type shit. Except the song would be going out of order in their situation.

"You one dawg ass nigga and I can't believe I'm having a baby by your ass," she spat with malice laced in her tone.

The statement had injured him, he felt as if she had just slapped him. Marcus wanted to respond but he bit into his bottom lip, opting to keep quiet. He wondered if she truly meant what she had just said. Marcus hoped that she didn't. He loved her and wanted his baby with her. From the moment he saw her, he knew that she would be the one to have all his kids. Leah had a pull on him so strong that he was scared if she let go, he would fall face first. He didn't want that. Marcus didn't want to know what life would be like without her. He needed to find some type of self-discipline and finally leave Chrissy alone. *It's just something about Chrissy though*, he thought. Reality hit him that he was torn between the two girls. He was in love with Leah, but Chrissy gave him a different feeling. She was willing to do whatever, whenever. However, Leah came with standards and wasn't willing to put up with him having this girl and that girl. She wanted him to be all hers and giving him a concubine would never be something she would allow.

"Mama," Marcus said.

"Don't call me that shit," she shouted.

He ignored her.

"Mama please stay. I can't be without you and I want to be with you and my baby," he said as he held his head down in shame.

Leah sighed, deep and long.

"You got one more time to put your hands on me or me catch you with another bitch and I promise it's over."

Marcus leaned up and kissed her softly. He vowed to himself to get this right. He didn't want to know what it would be like to not be with her. She was precious to him and was the only girl he ever loved. Yeah, Chrissy had been around, but he didn't love her. She was the one that he knew he could smoke with and fuck when he needed it. Leah provided something much different. She was smart and wanted to do better for herself and the people around her. They had spent countless nights talking about her dreams. Marcus admired her for the woman she wanted to become. The woman she was determined to become.

"Can you go get me food?" She asked as she laid down.

Marcus stood to his feet, grabbed his keys and headed out the door. He already knew what she wanted. Once Marcus left the room Leah cried a hard, ugly cry. She couldn't believe the things she was enduring. Putting up with all his bullshit because she wanted a family didn't seem worth the pain he caused. That was it, she didn't know *her* worth. She didn't realize that having a family didn't mean enduring physical trauma. Marcus was supposed to be her family, the one she felt safe with. Instead, she was scared and haunted. Leah closed her eyes as she rubbed her belly while whimpering until she fell asleep.

CHAPTER SIXTEEN

☐

*A*ll four of the teens got together to help Tyson and NuNu move into their new place on a Saturday morning. The weather was still cold but winter was almost over as they were climbing into the middle of February. The girls had searched for apartments every day for the past two months. NuNu received a call first and hurriedly paid the deposit and got her keys.

Leah also received a call for getting approved for one of the new homes that were built throughout the south side of Toledo. However, she would be waiting to move, she had decided that living with Marcus would be scary so she would be secretly moving on her own. She didn't want to take any chances. They were in a good space, but cohabitating wasn't the best move for them. Tyson rented a U-Haul to move NuNu's brand new bedroom set from her mom's house and all the baby things they had been purchasing throughout her entire pregnancy, including a new bedroom set for their princess as well. Tyson spared no expense when it came to his two ladies especially since money was flowing like water lately the way he and Marcus were running. Pulling up to their three bedroom home NuNu smiled as she climbed out the U-Haul first. She waddled to the door, the further along she got in her pregnancy, the slower she got. Tyson watched her from the truck, biting into his lip, as he wondered how did he get so damn lucky to have her. He finally climbed out, strolled up the walkway and stood behind her.

"What are you waiting for, baby girl?" He asked, leaning into her ear and planting a kiss there. NuNu held the key inside the door not believing how real this was becoming. She now had her own place, she would be someone's mother in a little under two months all while still managing to get through school. It was all so overwhelming, and she needed a moment as she turned around facing him with tears in her eyes.

"Ty, I'm nervous baby," she said, burying her face in his chest.

He pulled back, lifting her chin and swiped at her tears.

"It's okay baby girl, you got this and I tell you every day that I got you, I got us!" He said pointing between them two and then down to their daughter.

His reassurance was all she needed to put confidence back into her. NuNu smiled and pecked his lips.

"I love you, big daddy."

Tyson's dick jumped. They way NuNu said big daddy always aroused him.

"Nu'Asia you know how I get when you call me that," he said.

She was putting him in a mood. However, Leah and Marcus were around so he couldn't make her squeal right now.

"Let's get in here baby and start getting it together. We home," he said with a wink.

NuNu turned to unlock the door and stepped inside. Their home was beautiful. They had three bedrooms, a living room, dining room and a family room that was connected to the kitchen leading to their patio. NuNu loved big spaces, so their home was perfect. NuNu and Leah had cleaned the day before after Leah got off from work, so all they needed to do was start setting things up as it came in. Tyson stepped in behind her.

"Now you can be as loud as you want to while I'm in that baby," he whispered as he licked her ear.

"Ty, don't even start or we will be breaking this house in without the furniture being moved in yet."

Tyson laughed. He could just imagine having NuNu bent over their countertop. The visual sent a spark down to his loins. He shook his head. Right now, wasn't the time to be imagining because he would be bringing it to reality if she didn't stop playing with him.

"Please don't," Leah called from behind overhearing their conversation as she stepped inside with Marcus following behind her.

NuNu laughed but once she saw Marcus she frowned and was annoyed immediately. She did not plan on seeing him and did not want to be in his presence. NuNu also wasn't fond of him and Leah being back together. She knew her friend deserved better. Tyson noticed the look on her face.

"Nu don't start. I need another male to help me with this shit and he's the only one I trust to know where I lay my head. Don't even pay him any attention," he said, pecking her lips.

NuNu rolled her eyes as she started running down orders on what she needed everyone to do. The boys unloaded the truck while the girls unloaded the cars that had the smaller stuff in them. NuNu had music bumping from their home stereo system as they danced all over the house while setting things up. They boys managed to bring in all the heavy items without denting or scratching up NuNu's walls because they knew she would have a fit. After everything was out of the U-Haul they left, leaving the girls to take of the rest.

"Leah do you think it's a good idea for you and Marcus to live together? Or better yet even be together?" NuNu asked as she started placing candles on her end tables for decoration. Leah sighed not wanting to have this conversation, but she knew it was soon to come, so she might as well get it over with now.

"Nu, even though I want to give my baby a two-parent home, I don't plan to move in with him. But as far as us being together Nu, we're fine,"

"For how long Leah, how long before you catch him cheating? And let's not mention that new fucking bruise under your eye that you think I didn't peep," NuNu interrupted.

She didn't like Marcus and she had no shame in hiding the feeling. She looked at her friend filled with disappointment because Leah had been reduced down to the girl that would tolerate anything just to have a family. Leah placed a finger to the exact spot where she knew the knot was and rubbed there as her mind flashed back to that day she got it.

199

"Why the fuck you turn your phone off?" Marcus asked. He backed Leah up against the door trapping her face in the U of his hand. "I had exams today and I needed to study, without any distractions," Leah said as her heart raced. Marcus was upset and she could tell if she didn't try to calm him down and get him to understand that she needed to focus, it would get worse. Leah had turned her phone off over the weekend only accepting calls from NuNu because she had her godmother's phone number. She was focusing. However, her wanting to do so caused an issue with Marcus. He popped up at her school and took her back to his house. Now here he was in her face, fuming. "So, you couldn't study here?" He barked. Marcus back handed Leah. She slid to the floor crying. This was what she wanted to avoid. "Marcus, please. You tripping for nothing. How are you mad cause I wanted to focus?" She buried her face in her hands. "Just say you was with a nigga. Why else would you turn your phone off?" He was now accusing her of cheating and Leah couldn't believe her ears.

"Leah," NuNu called out. Leah snapped out of her thoughts. She sighed.

"Nu, we're good," Leah started to explain.

"No, you are not Leah Bre'Ana, you deserve better sister and I hate seeing you like this. I hate that nigga and wish we would have never crossed his path." NuNu stated.

Leah swiped away at a tear that was trailing down the right side of her face. NuNu walked over to her and hugged her tightly.

"I'm sorry, I just want better for you and you should want better for you as well," she said as she took a step back and looked at Leah in the eyes.

"I know," Leah whispered as she held her head down and started fidgeting with the gold *L* that rested on her right hand.

NuNu knew once she did that she was on the verge of shutting down so she changed the subject. The conversation had gotten heavy and she didn't want a somber mood to come over them both.

"Come on heffa lets go set up your god daughter room while these damn boys are still gone."

The girls had put a portable cd player in the baby's room and were listening to mixed cd's as they laid her room out in Minnie Mouse themed decor. Leah had found alphabet letters for them to paint and hang up that spelled out Ma'Leah's name. Once they were finished with the baby's room, they moved to NuNu and Tyson's. Thank god the boys had done all the hard work and all the girls had to do was make the king size bed and put away all clothing and shoes.

"When do you find out what you are having?" NuNu asked as she folded Tyson's shorts and placed them on his side of the dresser.

"Here, soon. I got back to the doctors in two weeks," Leah replied.

"Any names picked out?" NuNu quizzed.

"Well if it's a boy I'm going to name him Markest Anthony and Marcus said if it's a girl he wants her name to be Ma'Laysia Bre'Ana."

NuNu pushed the drawer closed and turned from the dresser with shocked eyes. Marcus had to know that the baby

201

name was a part of hers and it made her feel special. NuNu held a hand to her chest as she smiled. She crossed the room and pulled Leah in for a hug.

"I still don't like his ass, so I hope he don't think this is going to win me over," she said as she went back to folding her man clothes.

*A*fter Tyson and Marcus dropped the truck off, they popped in Tyson's car and headed to the block. On the way there Marcus looked over to Tyson.

"Man, Nu really hates me huh?" He asked.

Tyson laughed at the rhetorical question and nodded. Marcus laughed as well and shook his head. He knew she couldn't stand him. She didn't hide her distaste for him at all. NuNu was just as blunt as they come. She said what she wanted, there was no sugar coating with her.

"She's mean as fuck dawg, how the hell do you deal with her?" Marcus asked. Tyson grinned. He didn't think she was mean, he just knew she didn't bite her tongue or take shit from no one.

"The person she gives y'all and the person she gives me is different. She's tough with y'all but with me, she's both tough and soft. I love the combination she gives me cause the mean side makes a nigga weak at times." Tyson replied.

"Whatever you say big dawg," Marcus shot back.

"But let me ask you this," Tyson said as he pulled over in front of City's crib.

Since they were in the line of asking questions, Tyson had a few of his own. There were things about Marcus he didn't understand, things that he didn't approve of when it came to the way he treated Leah. She was his sister and he was his boy. They had formed a bond but protecting Leah would always come before their bond.

"Why do you be treating Leah like that man? That shit ain't cool at all and I'm surprised she hasn't had one of her uncles, step to you yet."

Marcus sat there for a moment. The question had taken him by surprise. He felt like he was getting ready to answer to her father, the way Tyson was looking at him. *Damn, why do I treat her like that?* He thought.

"Truth be told I don't even know dawg," Marcus replied.

"Then you be cheating and hitting on her while she pregnant nigga that shit really ain't cool." Tyson continued.

He didn't understand Marcus's ways of thinking when it came to women. *I could never treat Nu'Asia like that*, he thought to himself.

"Hold up nigga don't act like you don't be cheating on NuNu's mean ass, you're not Mr. faithful," Marcus said laughing.

Tyson sat there with a straight face. He didn't find amusement in Marcus's statement. He wasn't a cheater. Cheating on NuNu had never crossed his mind. He gave her his all and she was all he needed. She fed him in ways no other girl had. It was like she made love to his soul. Yeah, she was mean, but he loved her regardless. So, to cheat on her was a no go. What he did as a single man was different, but while in a relationship he was solid. He was a firm believer in treating a woman how he wanted his mother to be treated. Marcus noticed his seriousness. He was sitting before a man. Tyson wasn't some street boy that went around rounding up girls just to have a line up, especially not while he was committed.

"Naw dummy, I don't and I don't plan on it. Don't get me wrong bitches approach me all the time and be pitching the pussy at me all the fucking time dawg. However, I can't see her cry because of me so I could never do anything that I know will lead to that." Tyson said.

Marcus sat back in his seat in deep thought. Tyson was spitting free game, hoping Marcus was soaking it up and hopefully would apply it to his and Leah relationship.

"Damn that's wassup homie. I wish I had the self-discipline you got cause I can only run away from it for so long before I catch myself knocking some shit out the park," Marcus said with a smirk.

"Man shut your punk ass up and go get that money from City's weird ass," Tyson said chuckling.

Marcus laughed as he got out of the car. His boy had him pondering on the notion of being fully committed. Could he be that type of nigga for Leah? He had told her before that he never had a serious girlfriend, this relationship thing was foreign to him. He didn't have a father around to teach him the blueprint on how to treat women. He just guessed, so was

204

he truly the blame for how he treated her? Marcus shook the thought from his head as he continued up the walkway and focused back on business.

Tyson sat there waiting for Marcus as he thumbed through the money he had laying in his lap. Them hitting licks and flipping bricks was doing them good as Tyson saw his pockets swell quicker from picking up the extra work. He turned up the radio as Juvenile *400 Degrees* slumped through his speakers. Keeping an eye open always, he scanned his surroundings and noticed a hooded figure approaching his car from the passenger side mirror and then switched to the other side approaching the driver's side. *Who the fuck is this?* he thought as he squinted his eyes watching his mirror. Tyson reached under the seat quickly grabbing his gun, took it off safety and slammed the door into the person as they approached. The dude went flying to the cement as Tyson hopped out and pointed his pistol at him.

"Take ya fucking hood off homie," Tyson barked.

"Yo Tyson, It's me Dominic man," he said while holding up one hand and taking his hood off with the other.

"Nigga, what the fuck you doing creeping up on my shit?" Tyson said as he saw Marcus emerging from the house.

"Ty, I don't want no beef with you, I know you said we still got problems but I just want to walk around my hood in peace and not worry about catching fades with you and Marcus."

Tyson grabbed the hand that Dominic was holding up and pulled him to his feet. Tyson was older, 22 and now becoming a father. Beefing with a little nigga like Dominic was the last thing on his mind.

"Aye, listen you good my way home boy but don't ever text my lady again. The same way you just rolled up on me trying to make peace is the same way you could have sent that apology to Nu, *through me!*"

"My fault," Dominic said.

Tyson shook his head, he couldn't believe how scary the dude was. Marcus eyed him still wanting beef. Tyson saw it in his face however, he wasn't about to let an unnecessary scene be caused over some shit that happened months ago.

"Dummy get in the car and let this nigga be," Tyson said, tapping his chest and then climbing back in his car.

Marcus nodded his head, went to the passenger side and climbed in, leaving Dominic alone without a word being spoken.

Tyson turned to Marcus laughing as he started the ignition and pulled from the curb.

"Yo, I don't know what my baby girl saw in that short ass nigga. I'm glad she didn't give him no pussy and had let that shit marinate for a real nigga," he said smirking as he told Marcus to count up what he just collected.

*T*yson entered his home after NuNu had texted him, telling him to bring back shrimp fried rice from her favorite Chinese place and Uno cards. Of course, he always did what he was asked and was back home within 45 minutes. The boys returned with food, cards and orange juice for both girls.

"Ty, these not Uno cards, why did you get these?" NuNu whined as she pulled the cards out from the bag. Tyson shook his head. NuNu was a brat. His brat.

"They didn't have any baby girl, I'm sorry. I just got regular cards so we could just bust some spades instead."

NuNu looked to Leah and then back to Tyson as she pointed and mouth, "I don't want to be on her team."

Leah peeped the innuendo. She cocked her head back and put a hand on her hip.

"Bitch, I don't want to be on your team either."

NuNu hollered. She knew Leah would catch her talking shit. Leah couldn't play spades, so NuNu was serious about not wanting to be her partner. Leah always under bid not knowing what she had in her hand and NuNu wasn't down with losing tonight.

"Didn't nobody tell yo ass to be nosey Bre'Ana," NuNu said, calling Leah by her middle name like she was her mother.

Marcus cut in.

"How about we just be on our girl's team then?" He suggested.

NuNu cut her eyes at him and cringed, that's how much she couldn't stand him.

"Nobody asked you," NuNu snapped as she made her way to her dining room table. Marcus could do nothing but shake his head as they all paired off into partners and got the game going while they ate their food.

CHAPTER SEVENTEEN

☐

*A*week after moving into their house, NuNu and Tyson

laid in bed watching *The Fresh Prince of Bel-Air*. Tyson laid in NuNu's lap as she rested her head against the headboard enjoying the show. NuNu rubbed Tyson's head and pecked the side of it. She was glad he decided to stay in for the day. She had been missing him lately and wanted his company. Since finding out she was pregnant Tyson had been going hard. He was grinding, to get his cake up to make sure his family would always be straight. However, today would be all about NuNu and whatever she wanted to do. She looked down at him as she began to caress the side of his face.

"How does it feel having our own place?" She asked.

"It feels good baby girl," he responded, craning his neck up to peck her lips.

NuNu smiled. It felt good to her as well. They were able to lay around or walk through the house naked if they choose to. She no longer had to hear her mother's mouth about Tyson running in and out all times of the night. Tyson was respectful, he had always offered to stay at home with his mother if he knew he would be out late. However, NuNu insisted that he made sure he was in her presence when he went to bed at night, no matter how late it was. Moving out was inevitable, especially since they were expanding their family

"Ty, do you think we moved too fast?"

Tyson's eyebrows dipped in confusion at the thought of where the question had come from. "Naw, I don't think we moved too fast Nu'Asia, where did that even come from?" He asked. NuNu leaned back and sighed.

"I don't know I was just wondering since we only been together for a year and already having a baby and living together. You don't think this was all too soon?" Tyson lifted from her lap switching positions with her as he made her lay against his chest. He could tell she was overthinking and he needed to get her to relax before she started getting worked up. He took a deep breath and then kissed the top of her head.

"Nu'Asia we good, who cares how fast you got pregnant, who cares how fast we moved in together. All things happened for a reason and it was a reason for all of this. You're almost finished with school, so I see no issues there. Once the baby gets here, you'll be able to move how you always moved, just with a baby to motivate you to go hard in the paint, ya know?" NuNu nodded.

"I just don't want either one of us to regret any of this later on down the line Ty."

"We won't baby girl I promise," he said, kissing her cheek.

Tyson just had an aura about him. When he spoke, NuNu listened. She trusted what he said and knew that he wouldn't mislead her. It had been that way ever since the first day she laid eyes on him. Her heart yearned for him long before she built up the nerve to step to him. She now understood why other boys before him weren't worthy of her temple. It had been constructed for him and him only.

"Oh, and my mom's want you to come back over this Sunday for dinner," he said, changing the subject.

NuNu had met his mother on Christmas and the two women clicked instantly. NuNu smiled, she loved his mama. She loved her even more because she had created her equal and NuNu would forever be grateful for that. She made sure she had thanked her for making him. His mother was baffled by the comment. NuNu was bold and that's what made his mother like her. She wasn't afraid to speak her mind and Tyson's mother respected her.

"She said you thanking her for creating me is what made her like you," Tyson said smiling. "She was going to like me regardless," NuNu said, shrugging.

Tyson kissed the back of her head again. Silence fell over the room as they continued watching their show. The time they spent together had always been special. NuNu never moved from his chest, which was her favorite spot to be. It was her safe haven, she felt the most love when in that area.

"Ty," NuNu called out.

"What's up baby," he responded, still fixed in on the tv.

"You know I really don't like Marcus or the idea of you with him all the time," she stated. Tyson reached over to the nightstand to grab the remote and mute the show. He knew that the conversation was about to get severe and he wanted to give her his undivided attention.

"What you mean baby, you know we do business most of the time and the other times we with y'all. What is it not to like?" he asked, slightly bothered. NuNu knew they did business and Tyson had already told her, his business was the only thing she couldn't control.

"I know, but what if the shit he does makes you want to start doing it too?" she said lowly.

"Nu'Asia for the last time-"

"I know you are your own man," she said rolling her eyes.

Tyson removed himself from behind her and stood up pacing the floor. He swiped a hand down his face. Tyson let out an exasperated breath. NuNu stayed having him trying to defend his character. He was tired of having to tell her that he was his own man. *What the fuck I look like letting a nigga influence me*, he thought as he grew frustrated. "Man listen I swear it's like you want a nigga to fuck up or something," he said finally speaking with irritation in his tone.

"No, I don't want you to fuck up, I just know you use to having bops and that nigga stay cheating," she spat.

Tyson didn't miss the hidden insecurity. NuNu didn't want to end up like Leah, being cheated on. She was scared that a formidable day would come, and she wouldn't know how to handle it.

"Hell, you know the saying, birds of a fucking feather flock together." she continued.

"I DONT GIVE A…" Tyson caught himself yelling and shook his head. He took in a deep breath and then exhaled slowly.

"You know what, I'm not about to argue with you about this shit cause it's petty Nu'Asia." He had never raised his voice at her, and he wasn't about to start now. The fact that he was even about to, had him feeling disturbed on the

212

inside. *I got to show her what type of nigga dukes raised me to be*, he thought. He heard insecurity dripping from her tone but just as much as she was scared, he was too. Tyson often pondered on the day she would leave because of her thoughts of him being too good to be true. It terrified Tyson. He didn't want to be without her and noticing the issue she battled with about his love for her, let him know that he had to be patient with her. He had to do everything he could to rectify it. Tyson left their bedroom leaving NuNu to her thoughts.

When he got to the living room he went into the closet and grabbed down a black box that he had hidden. *I got to get her head off that shit once and for all*, he thought. He strolled over to their home stereo system and flipped through the cd case, finding a mixed cd that he had just purchased with a few songs that he knew NuNu would love. "Fuck," he said under his breath as he went back to the closet to get the plucked rose petals that he hid in there as well.

NuNu laid in the bed as she flipped through the channels of the tv in irritation. She couldn't believe that he had just left her sitting in the room without speaking another word. *The audacity of him*, she thought. Tyson had her fucked up if he was just going to go to a different part of the house without talking to her. "You know what, we are about to finish this damn conversation," she mumbled, tossing the remote on the nightstand as she stood from the bed. As if Tyson could read her mind, he called for her to come to him. She slipped on her house shoes and waddled her pregnant behind down the stairs but froze when she heard music playing. *What the...*

213

If loving you is all that I have to do
I don't want to do anything else
If loving you is all that I have to do
I don't want to do anything else

What in the hell is he doing? She thought as she finished descending the stairs. Tyson had scattered the rose petals from the last step to the middle of the living room floor where a big silver rug stretched across the floor. Mary J. Blige feat Jodeci was playing from their speakers as she made her way to where he was standing with his arms open as he sang to her.

Every night and day, I dream of another way
To tell you something good, I don't think that I'm
understood
You walk away and I frown, with my head hung far down
You tell me what is wrong, do you just want to be loved all
night long baby

NuNu smiled from ear to ear as she watched him sing to her. His shirt was off and his tattooed covered body was on full display. He looked damn good to her at that moment. Well, in every moment but this scene playing in front of her put the icing on the cake cause this nigga was spilling his soul.

"What are you doing?" she asked, laughing as she walked up to him.

He pulled her into him and they slowly danced as Tyson put his moves down like he was one of them damn boys from

214

Jodeci. NuNu hollered in laughter as she encouraged him to keep going.

"Aww shit daddy," she said as she held one arm up snapping her fingers.

Tyson had to laugh at that. He stopped, went to turn the music down a bit, and put the song on repeat. He approached NuNu and took her in for a moment. She was so beautiful. He had to let it be known that he had tunnel vision and the only girl he could see was her. *Only if lor mama knew what she truly means to me,* he thought as he shook his head.

"What is it baby?" she asked, noticing his gaze lasting longer than usual.

"Nu'Asia all bullshit to the side and please just listen. Don't take this shit the wrong way." he started.

"What is it Ty?" she pushed.

"I got plenty of bitches that want to suck this dick."

NuNu turned to head back up the stairs cause she didn't even want to hear shit else but he stopped her, grabbing her by the arm and forcing her to listen.

"Listen, baby girl, I'm serious. I got plenty of skuzzies wanting this dick but all I want is YOU! I don't want anyone but your mean ass and my daughter," he said sincerely.

NuNu eyes began to water because as the words to the song continued to play she caught on to where he was going. Tyson continued.

"I just want you Nu'Asia, you make me whole and without you I'm incomplete. Just please let me keep loving you. You're it for me cause no one else will do."

He lowered to one knee and pulled a box from his shorts pocket. NuNu's eyes widened and her hands went to her mouth in shock. She grew weak in the knees again, just like the first day she approached him at the park.

"Nu'Asia Marie Collins will you please be a nigga wife?"

NuNu cried from her soul at the sound of those words and nodded her head. Tyson bit into those pink lips of his. He was gracious that she had agreed, placing the 3ct ring on her finger and came up off his knees to kiss her. NuNu couldn't control her tears, she was so overwhelmed as they hugged and she stared at her hand. The ring was beautiful. Flawless. *When did he even have time to plan this? This can't be real. He couldn't be serious right now.* She thought. NuNu's mind was racing so fast she couldn't keep up. Tyson couldn't possibly want her to be his wife. It was too soon. But shit she wanted to be his wife. She wanted to be the only woman he would ever love because she was certain that he would be the only man she would ever love.

"Are you serious?" she said as she pulled away from him. As Tyson was nodding his response NuNu passed out. "BABYGIRL!.."

Leah and Marcus walked the aisles of KMART, shopping for baby clothes and going back and forth about who they thought the baby would look like. "She is going to look like her handsome dad," Marcus said, swiping a hand down his face as he looked in a mirror used for baby car seats. They had found out they were having a girl and Marcus was ecstatic about it. "Boy you can calm the hell down shit," Leah laughed as she scanned the racks for cute onesies.

"MaLaysia, you hear your dad out here acting a monkey and donkey right now," she said rubbing her stomach.

Marcus laughed as he approached Leah from behind while she looked for the clothes.

"I love you mama," Marcus said as he kissed her.

Marcus did in fact, love Leah with his entire heart. She was the only one for him but if presented with the opportunity he would betray her. He never did it out of intentions, it was the way he was. He believed that because he was young that he had his whole life to settle down and truly be faithful to her. He would keep her barefoot and pregnant raising his children, that way he knew she wouldn't flee. She wanted her children to all have the same father and be raised in a two parent family home just as he did. She believed strongly in that. Leah would endure whatever to make sure that type of lifestyle was provided for her daughter and the children that would follow.

"Love you too," she said back. They walked over to the car seat and stroller area and came across a black and pink seat that Leah absolutely loved.

"Ooh look, chocolate man, it comes in a combo and it is on sale."

"We ain't getting shit if you don't stop calling me chocolate man, you know I don't like that shit." Leah laughed. She knew he hated it but that's who he was her chocolate man. Marcus picked the box up and placed it in the cart.

"Man, I don't want to put this shit together," he said as he looked at the box seeing that it didn't come already assembled.

Leah rolled her eyes.

"Lazy ass," she mumbled under her breath.

"Shit call it what you want," he shot back.

Marcus wasn't the handyman type. He wasn't good at following directions and always paid his little homies to put something together for him. Leah thought just maybe he needed to see someone else do it and then he'd catch on but no he was just plain useless when it came to handy work.

"Uncle Ty will put it together," she said indirectly.

"He will have to cause I ain't," Marcus said as he pushed the cart over to the sock and t-shirt area. He was annoyed. Leah was always talking slick shit underneath her breath and being indirect. He believed that's why they always had issues that caused him to lay hands on her. *She always got smart shit to say.*

"And you can go somewhere with all that slick shit you talking, too," he voiced.

"Whatever," she said as she followed behind him reaching inside her Coach purse for her ringing phone. "Speaking of the devil," she said.

"What's up Ty?" she said stopping in the middle of the aisle at the alarm in his voice.

"SHE WHAT?" Leah yelled.

Leah caught Marcus's attention and he turned around in concern.

"What's wrong mama? Everything okay?" He asked.

"We have to go," she said as she pushed the cart out the way.

"Ok let me pay for this shit real quick," he said, grabbing the cart.

"NO.! Let's fucking go now. Nu had the baby," she screamed.

Leah entered Toledo Hospital heading to the third floor where the labor and delivery was. She stepped off the elevator and rounded the corner to the front desk. She approached the counter where a middle age white woman sat holding a phone to her ear.

"How can I help you?" the lady sitting at the desk asked.

"Yes, I need Nu'Asia Collins room number please," Leah said.

"Oh, she can't have visitors at the moment until the doc--."

"Bitch, I don't give a fuck what the doctor got to do I'm going in there to see my sister and god daughter," Leah spat cutting the lady off.

"Mama chill," Marcus said as he wrapped an arm around her waist. The nurse was stunned by Leah's outburst. Leah's hormones had her going crazy. Being told she couldn't see her best friend wasn't the right answer, so the woman caught an explosive attitude in return.

"Ma'am I'm sorry but…"

Leah saw Tyson coming out of the room and dismissed whatever it was the lady was about to say.

He guided them to her room. Leah stepped in laying watery eyes on NuNu as she laid in the bed sleeping. She

219

noticed the baby sound asleep in the bassinet beside NuNu's bed. Leah approached NuNu kissing her forehead and then turned to the sleeping baby.

"Oh my god Ty, she is so freaking pretty and small."

"He!" Tyson corrected.

"What?" Leah said as she looked down at the baby again.

"You heard me right," Tyson said as he shook his head.

This whole time they thought they were having a girl, it turned out they were having a boy. The nurse that had given them a false gender was new and didn't realize that the baby had his legs crossed. After giving birth to the baby NuNu had unkind words for that nurse who had just so happened to be assisting the doctor with the birth.

"Had me calling my lor baller princess and shit." Tyson scoffed.

"Hi, baby Ty," Leah cooed.

Her god baby was a spitting image of his dad. Tyson couldn't deny him. Baby Tyson had his father's whole face and Leah couldn't believe it. He had the juiciest cheeks she had ever seen, and the cutest dimple rested on his left cheek.

"You sure you're not the one that carried him Ty?" she said as she went to reach for him. "Wash your hands before you pick him up Leah," Tyson said as he rubbed NuNu head climbing in the bed next to her.

"Sorry, sorry, sorry," Leah said as she headed for the sink in the room.

"Congrats dawg," Marcus said walking up to Tyson and dapping him up.

"Thanks, homie."

Leah returned from washing her hands picking up Baby Ty as her heart immediately swelled.

She fought back tears of emotions. Her best friend was now a mother and her god son was perfect.

"Ty, how in the world was he born so early," Leah quizzed.

"He was technically only born 2 weeks early. The doctors had his timing off somehow."

"How big was he and what's his length?

"He was 6lbs and 7oz and 19in long," Tyson replied.

"JuRell god mommy so in love with you and I've only known you all but 5 minutes," Leah said, calling him by his middle name.

Tyson smiled, it made him feel good knowing that his lady had a friend like Leah. He then nudged NuNu awake, she had wanted him to wake her once Leah got there and he knew if he let her stay asleep she would throw a fit. NuNu's eyes fluttered open as she groaned. NuNu looked to the left and smiled as she saw Leah sitting in a reclining chair next to her holding her son. Leah looked up.

"Hi Heffa, how are you feeling?" she asked. Leah was filled with questions.

It was going to be her turn soon and she wanted to be prepared for what she had involuntarily signed up for.

"My pussy hurt, it feels like he split me right in half," NuNu said.

"Nu'Asia your mouth we got other people in here." Tyson warned.

NuNu looked toward the door noticing Marcus standing there on his phone.

"What he…"

She stopped herself and rolled her eyes she didn't have the energy to even ask what the fuck he was doing there knowing she didn't like him. Tyson whispered in her ear for her to be cool and relax. She whispered back, "this nigga knows I can't fucking stand his dawg ass, Ty."

"Okay, baby girl we know but you got to chill you just went through a rough 3 hours." "Okay baby," she whispered, putting her head back against the pillow.

"Leah can you hand me the cup of water sitting right there on that tray?" NuNu asked.

Her mouth felt like cotton and she felt dehydrated. Leah lifted carefully making sure she didn't move too fast and disrupt the baby's sleep. She handed NuNu the cup, noticing the ring on NuNu's finger and her eyes widened.

"Um, Nu'Asia Marie what the fuck is that on your hand?" she asked.

NuNu smirked.

"Yeah, bitch I locked that nigga all the way down now," she said, sticking out her tongue. Leah hollered laughing.

Tyson shook his head and kissed her. She was so damn cocky and arrogant. "Naw, I locked you down the moment I bust all in you and created my world," he said, smirking.

NuNu's face turned hot, his mannish mouth had always been her favorite thing. Tyson was a pretty boy and his filthy talk always stirred something in her. *This boy's fucking mouth is what led me here in the first place,* she thought. The entire room shared a laugh at his response before Leah asked when it all happened.

"Girl he did the cutest thing ever after we had a disagreement. I came downstairs and the nigga was singing to me," NuNu said.

"Awwww Ty," Leah laughed.

"He asked, I said yeah. Then I remember asking him if it was real and passed out after. That's what sent me into labor," NuNu told her as she took a sip of water.

"Can you believe he came out a boy?" Leah asked.

"Girl I cussed that damn nurse out when she came in here," NuNu said, shaking her head. "We bought all that girl stuff just to have a boy instead."

"Well since we're having a girl, I'll take that stuff and will go get boy stuff for baby Ty," Leah said looking down at him.

"JuRell," Leah cooed to her god son again. She was so in love with him already and could only imagine how it would be once Ma'Laysia arrived.

CHAPTER EIGHTEEN

☐

*L*eah wiped the dining area tables off at work as she waited for her shift to end. She had been texting NuNu all day bugging her about what the baby was doing. She always got the same response. "We laying down trying to rest Leah damn," NuNu would say.

Leah couldn't help but be excited, she was crazy about her god son and forever wanted to be over there with him if she wasn't busy with work or homework. Baby Ty was 3 weeks old and had everyone wrapped around his pinky, especially Leah and Tyson. Tyson didn't stand a chance, his heart always raced when he was around his son.

Leah heard a group of boys entering the restaurant. She looked up and saw Dominic. They locked eyes briefly. Leah hadn't seen him around since the day Marcus had pulled up on them, acting a fool. She waved and continued to wipe down the tables. Dominic swaggered over to her and Leah froze. Flashes of Mandy popped in her head.

"What's up Leah?" He asked.

"Oh, hey Nic," she said.

Being in Dominic's presence was overwhelming. She felt like she couldn't breathe. Leah wanted to run out of the building. She could no longer look him in his eyes, knowing what she had done to cause him heartache.

"How have you been Nic?" She asked as if she didn't already know. She knew he was heartbroken. He looked different. Dominic had bags under his eyes like he hadn't slept in forever. He no longer held his athletic frame, he was smaller. Mandy's death had taken a toll on him as well as their unborn child.

"Do you even need to ask? I barely sleep, I drink all the time. Shits fucked up Leah, and to top it off I constantly get random text from an unknown number that freaks me the fuck out." He said.

Leah was confused. *What the hell does he mean he gets random texts*, she thought. Leah needed answers but before she was able to interrogate him, his crew beckoned for him to roll out. Dominic looked at her, shook his head and stepped without another word. Leah felt her emotions starting to build up. She quickly stifled them as she pulled out her phone to check the time.

Marcus walked in as she slid her phone in her pocket and wiped the last table for the night. Leah couldn't even muster up a genuine smile like she usually did when she saw him. They had been going through it lately. Him still cheating and her always forgiving when he came back to say I'm sorry. Leah wasn't herself, she was unhappy. She always wanted to be around NuNu and Baby Tyson, they brought warmth and light to her cold and dark days.

"What's crackin' mama?" he called to her as he approached the table.

"Hey chocolate man," she said as she leaned in to kiss his lips.

"You ready to bounce?" he asked as he went to get her bookbag from the normal spot she kept it in.

"Yeah," she replied as she went around the counter to clock out.

"Leah, we need you to run the back window for about 15 minutes please," Daynice called from the manager's office.

Leah rolled her eyes as she made her way back up front to tell Marcus she would be no more than 20 minutes. She knew he would be pissed. He got mad over everything lately and she was emotionally drained. She dreaded having to tell him she needed to stay longer.

"Damn, man you should have told her ass no or something, shit," he said as he pulled out his phone checking the time and message that had just made his phone vibrate.

"Who is that?" she asked.

She had noticed the corners of his mouth turn up a tad bit too much for her liking. *I'm so sick of this shit.*

"Don't fucking worry about it, just hurry up man I'll be waiting in the car," he barked as he turned to make his exit.

Leah went to grab his phone and he snatched back from her. She was tired of playing games with him, tired of enduring pain when it came to love he was claiming to give.

"What the fuck you mean don't worry about it?"

She tried to whisper but her words came out louder than expected. She didn't want to cause a scene, but she had a feeling one was about to be made. Marcus was up to his normal cheating ways. Leah was fed up. She was tired, mentally and physically tired of his bullshit. It was never ending.

"Leah gone some fucking where! Don't they still need you?" He asked. He tried to block her attempts to get his phone as held his phone in one hand and pushed Leah with the other.

"Marcus what the fuck are you on?" she yelled.

She no longer cared who heard her or who may have been watching. She wanted answers and refused to let him continue to toy with her. Marcus looked around as he pulled her towards the restrooms. He pushed her roughly into the corner. He grabbed her by the face forcefully and pinned her against the wall.

"Aight man you can chill with all the rowdy shit, don't fucking embarrass me and I'm not on shit," he spat.

"Marcus, get your fucking hands off me," she said softly.

He had her jaws pinched so tight her mouth was watering as her teeth started cutting into her cheeks. He was up to something and she felt it in her soul. *Every fucking time I turn around this nigga doing something, he doesn't give a fuck how this is making me feel,* she thought. "Now, like I fucking said, I'll be waiting in the car, so hurry up cause I got shit to do."

He didn't notice the tall dude leaving at the same time he was and bumped right into him. "Dang my fault homie," Marcus said as he turned to face the boy. "It's all good," the tall boy shot back as he turned around at the sound of the cashier calling his name.

Marcus exited the building and Leah wiped at her face pulling herself together. *He always talking about he got shit to do,* she thought. She headed back around to the dining area and bumped into the same guy Marcus had just ran into.

227

"Excuse me," she said as she tried to go around him.

"If you were my lady I would never talk to you like that," he said.

He had heard their altercation since he was the last customer placing an order inside.

"Well, I'm not your lady and it's not your business," she spat, still trying to get past him.

"I'm Jamison," he said, offering her a name as he stared at her and was not at all bothered by the attitude.

"Well Jamison *I'm busy* and need to get back to work," Leah stated.

"Okay *Leah*," he said as he moved out of her way,

"I'll be seeing you again so make sure you remember me."

He made his exit and Leah went back to the office. *Wait a minute, how in the hell did he know my name?* she thought before she entered the office. Leah looked down at her uniformed perturbed. She wasn't wearing her name tag and couldn't recall ever seeing him before. *Who the hell is he?* she pondered.

"Leah gone ahead and clock out and take your drama with you," Daynice told her as she approached her.

Her boss's voice distracted her from her thoughts.

"I'm sorry he just-"

"You ain't gotta explain nothing to me," her manager said, stopping her.

"I'll get someone to cover your shift tomorrow, so don't worry about coming in," she told her before heading to the drive-thru window. Leah clocked out and grabbed her coat off the rack. Before making her way to the front Daynice stopped her, grabbing Leah by the hand, leading her back to the office. Daynice closed the door as they both sat down. Leah braced herself for what was about to be said. She just knew she was about to be fired for the drama that had occurred.

"The way you two were going at it is ridiculous. First of all, you're pregnant and you don't need that stress on you or your baby. Second, you're too pretty for the bruises that I keep seeing appear on your face. Ain't no nigga or no dick that damn good that you keep enduring him putting his damn hands on you. He is weak and you make him feel strong when you allow him to knock you down. You're worth more Leah, you deserve more, and he doesn't deserve you."

Leah was a mess, snot and tears were streaming down her face and her chest rocked from the way she had begun to cry. Daynice had given Leah a raw uncut version as if she was her mama and wanted to protect her. Daynice grabbed up some Kleenex and handed them to her to wipe her face. "Calm yourself down and stop crying baby girl," she said as she stood embracing Leah. "You're going to be okay and once you realize you're better off without him the better off you'll be."

Leah stabled herself and hugged her boss. "Thank you, I needed that," she said as she made her departure.

uNu and Baby Tyson had been home for three weeks. Somehow NuNu ended up sick. She was miserable and could barely get out of bed. Tyson called her mom asking her if she could keep Baby Ty overnight so that NuNu could rest. And hopefully, feel better. He had things lined up that he needed to attend to, so her help was much needed. Ms. Andrea was excited and agreed and in the same breath had told them both that they bet not be going half on another damn baby. NuNu wasn't with sending her baby with anyone so soon. However, she knew she at least needed the night to try and get some sleep. She needed to get well because she for sure didn't want her son getting sick. So, for the baby's sake, she obliged. Tyson dropped the baby off earlier that day and came right back home to her. He was annoying her with wanting to be up under her. She needed him out of her face so he wouldn't get sick either.

She requested that he go chill with the boys as she took the day to rest and medicate herself. NuNu had been in the house all day by herself as she slept on and off throughout the day. She woke up to a text from Leah and Tyson, they both were checking in on her. She dozed off again this time when she woke up it was two in the morning. She looked to her left and Tyson wasn't home. *I know this nigga not still out*, she thought. Tyson never stayed out that late, he always came home to his lady at a decent hour. NuNu's internal alarm instantly started going off. She grabbed her phone and dialed his number. No answer. *Is this nigga getting on one with me?* She pondered as she dialed his number again. She paced the floor as the phone rang and then went to voicemail. NuNu looked at the phone and scoffed. Yeah, he had her fucked up. It was two in the morning. He wasn't in their bed and he wasn't answering the phone. She went over to her dresser and threw on a pair of his sweats and a hoodie, her fighting gear cause she was about to scrape a bitch behind this nigga. NuNu rubbed vaseline on her face and then slid into some all black forces as she made her way out the bedroom. Descending the stairs, she entered the living room and her heart skipped a beat. Tyson was laid out on the couch with his son on his chest sleeping. Tyson couldn't be away from him so after he had picked Marcus and his two cousins up from getting pulled over, he went and grabbed *his world* as he called him and came home. He had attempted to take Marcus and his people to Marcus's house, but Marcus mama locked everyone out. NuNu's entire heart swelled at the sight of them as she felt silly because her crazy ass was standing there with a greasy face and wearing fighting clothes for no reason. She shook her head. She wanted to kiss them both but opted not to and turned to go back upstairs.

"*Ohhh Marcus.*"

"What the fuck?" NuNu said as she made her way to the basement door. She thought she was tripping as she placed an ear to the basement door.

"I bet your baby mama don't be fucking you like this."

This nigga has lost his fucking mind, she thought as she put hurried feet against her carpet and ran straight to her room and grabbed her phone. It was almost 2:30 in the morning and she was sure Leah was asleep but she called

231

anyway. The phone just rang as she burned holes in the floor from pacing.

"Pick up the fucking phone Leah," she said as the phone went to voicemail for the third time.

"Fuck this shit," she said to herself as she raced down the stairs swiping up her keys and ran out the door.

NuNu didn't even put a coat on. She was going to get Leah and they were about to tear some shit up. She drove the 10 minutes to Leah's god mom's house and hoped out running to the door.

KNOCK KNOCK KNOCK

Leah heard the door as she lifted from the couch where she was sleeping with her American History book in her hand. She walked toward the door yawning.

KNOCK KNOCK KNOCK KNOCK

"I'm coming shit," she called out.

She swung the door open without even asking who it was this late in the middle of the night.

"Nu what in the hell is wrong why you knocking at the damn door like that?" Leah snapped.

NuNu stepped inside.

"Get your shoes on bitch lets go," NuNu said with her hand raised and thumb pointing back toward the door.

Leah sprang into action after noticing what NuNu had on. That was one thing about them, they always followed suit with one another when it came down to getting busy and having to scrape bitches. Leah was already in sweats and a tank, so she slid on a pair of all white forces and Baby Phat coat and headed out the door.

"Bitch is it Marcus?" she stopped and asked as Deja Vu hit her. This is how the scene played out last time NuNu came to get her with her fighting clothes on. She knew it wasn't Tyson. Leah also knew it wasn't just some random encounter either.

"Get in," NuNu said as she climbed into the driver's side.

Leah wanted to protest but didn't and climbed in the car. NuNu burned rubber pulling off.

"What the fuck he do now Nu?" Leah asked as she leaned her head back and waited for the blow she knew was coming.

"He got some bitch at my house in the basement fucking," NuNu said shaking her head.

Leah snapped her neck in NuNu's direction.

"He what?" she said.

She needed NuNu to run that back because she just knew she didn't hear her correctly. Marcus had lost his mind. He had no regards for Leah. The things he was taking her through didn't seem to matter to him. He moved how he wanted to and when he wanted to. He didn't care how it made her feel or how it made her look. Marcus had Leah looking stupid in front of her own friends. Marcus had crossed the line tonight. To have a girl in Leah's best friend's basement screamed disrespect. It screamed that he had NuNu fucked up. It was no way she was about to allow him to flat out disrespect her or her friend.

"Yeah you heard me right Leah and I swear if you don't leave that nigga alone after this, I'm beating your ass after you have my god daughter cause this nigga ain't shit. This nigga beyond fucking bold for that shit and I'm about to beat

233

her ass and his for the disrespect to my house and you.?" NuNu barked.

Leah sat in her seat, mouth agape. She didn't believe what she was hearing. She couldn't believe it. *He can't be this damn disrespectful*, she thought. Leah couldn't hide her emotions as she began to cry. Her chest felt heavy and she felt like she needed to vomit. Her baby girl started moving around, stretching her stomach. Leah placed her hand to her belly and rubbed as she tried to calm both her baby and her sickness.

"You know what take me back home I don't give a fuck no more," Leah said as she wiped at her wet face.

NuNu did not respond and just kept driving cause, either way, the girl was getting her ass beat. Leah would just have to be her cheerleader because there was no way she was letting this shit slide. Leah leaned her head against the window and her mind raced as she thought about all the shit he had been putting her through. She thought about how he had her out there looking stupid and it pissed her off.

"Matter of fact Nu I got this. I'm about to tear this bitch up and whatever I break I'll replace."

NuNu smirked while pulling up to her home. That's the Leah she needed to hear cause the one that was trying to be cool, calm, and collected wasn't working for her. They both climbed out and made their way up the walkway. NuNu was on the porch in seconds, Leah was getting bigger she couldn't move as quickly as she used to.

"Bitch hurry up," NuNu said with a smile as she watched her friend waddle.

NuNu unlocked the door and put a finger to her lips, instructing Leah to be quiet.

"They're in the basement, but Ty is on the couch with the baby. I'm about to make them go upstairs and when I come back down, we'll go down there," she whispered.

Leah nodded.

"Leah don't fucking move, you pregnant and I don't want shit to happen to you. Just watch me beat her ass for you." NuNu coached. Leah nodded again disregarding what was said cause she meant what she said. She was about to fuck some shit up. NuNu tapped Tyson lightly as she removed the baby from his chest. "Let's go upstairs baby," she whispered, putting the receiving blanket over her shoulder and placing little Tyson against it. NuNu ascended the stairs with Tyson swaggering behind her.

Once Leah heard Tyson hit the top step, she took off down the basement steps. She reached the bottom step and froze. Her heart galloped as she watched the girl on her knees sucking *her* cheating ass, dawg ass nigga's dick. Marcus was fisting the girl's braids as she was rocking his mic like she was auditioning to be a part of a girls group. Marcus let out a grunt and Leah saw red. She ran up and kicked the girl without deviation in the face.

"Bitch," Leah screamed as she turned around and slapped the fuck out of Marcus.

She slapped the nigga so quick and hard that it caught him off guard and caused him to stumble. NuNu ran up two piecing the girl that was trying her hand at catching Leah off guard.

"Bitch you must be silly," NuNu said as she dropped the girl from the blow that connected with her chin.

Tyson was right behind NuNu. She couldn't hide the fact that something was up. The duo was back in action dawg walking shit as the boys tried to break it up. "Nu'Asia." Tyson barked. NuNu steeled. She had been busted trying to be slick thinking Tyson wouldn't sniff her out. Marcus swooped Leah up and carried her up the stairs. He couldn't believe he had been so careless and got caught up.

"Chill mama you are pregnant and if something happens to my baby it's going to be a problem," he said.

Leah recoiled. *Is this nigga fucking serious?*

"The only problem we got is your slick dick that you can't keep to yourself. Fuck you. WE'RE DONE!"

He had some nerves. He was the one cheating and beating on her, so how could he even fix his mouth to say *if something happened to my baby*. His laying hands on her and having sex with other girls could very much be the cause of something happening to their baby. Leah was a wreck. She swiped NuNu's car keys and took off out the door, leaving Marcus standing there stupefied.

CHAPTER NINETEEN

$\mathcal{T}$he next morning NuNu sat in the rocking chair feeding Little Tyson as she waited for Tyson to wake up. Once the baby had finished his bottle NuNu put him on her shoulder and patted his back gently as she tried to get him to burp. Her mind raced as she thought about what had happened last night. The level of disrespect Marcus displayed to her, her home, and most importantly her best friend had NuNu in a mood. She didn't appreciate the behavior from him or Tyson. She couldn't believe he would allow some shit like that. She had went to sleep with a heavy heart and not talking to him.

"Burp for mama," NuNu said softly as she continued to pat the baby's back. She kissed the side of his cheek as he let out a loud burp causing him to cry. His cry stirred big Tyson out of his sleep and he searched for him.

"My world," Tyson called out.

Tyson sat up in bed and noticed them both in the rocking chair. He got up and strolled over to his baby boy and seized him from NuNu.

"Hold up," he said, giving him right back to his mother.

He went to the bathroom to wash his face and brush his teeth. He reentered the room, capturing his son and getting back in the bed.

"You feel better?" He asked NuNu.

He never took his eyes off his son. Baby Tyson was one of Tyson's biggest blessings. Even though Tyson thought he would be having a girl, he was happy that he had a son first. Tyson now had a little homie that he could ride around the city with. A replica of himself that he could bond with while they sat at the barbershop. His son was a mini version of him and he enjoyed seeing himself in his son.

"Yeah, I do," she replied, as she watched the most beautiful sight in front of her.

She loved the way Tyson loved their son and it caused her to get emotional every time they interacted. The vulnerable side he gifted to only his son somewhat made NuNu jealous. He loved her of course and was soft with her as well but a different side that NuNu had never seen before came out the day their baby boy was born. It was NuNu's first time seeing him cry as he held Little Tyson to his chest. His love for him was palpable for sure.

"I felt better after waking up last night," she continued.

"I'm glad," he said as he kissed his little man's forehead.

NuNu looked at them in awe. These were her boys and she loved them dearly. However, she needed to get some things off her chest. She needed to know why he would allow such disrespect to be brought to their home and towards Leah. Something like this is what brought out her insecurities. If Tyson would allow Marcus to disrespect Leah in front of him and not tell her, then he would do the same. However, she wouldn't just go around accusing him again or even trying to compare the two. But the thought... the horrible thought still lingered a like stain that was hard to get out of her favorite shirt.

"Ty, why would you let Marcus come here with a girl knowing…"

"Don't even think I'd allow some shit like that to happen Nu'Asia," he said in a low tone as he cut her off.

He called her by her full name, so she knew he wasn't playing around. Now the fact that he didn't raise his voice put her in a mood. Tyson's firm but gentle tone always set NuNu on fire. His calmness behind saying her first name made her want to pop some pussy for him. *I can't wait for these last few weeks to be over cause baby Ty going to have another sibling on the way*, she thought to herself.

"Well what happened Ty, how'd they end up here and fucking in my basement? We ain't even fucked in the basement yet." She said.

Ty looked up at her and smirked. That *yet* let him know she planned on sitting on top of the washer while it was on the spin cycle as he rocked in and out of her.

"Chill baby with that kind of talk. That nigga Marcus was on some clown shit, he told me that they were his cousins."

"They? Who else was here?" NuNu asked.

"It was him, a dude and the bop he smashed. I picked them up after he called me telling me they got pulled over and the car got towed. I tried to drop all their asses off at his house because I didn't want them mufuckas here, but his mom dukes was on one and locked them out. I went and got my world and we all came here. Next thing I know as I'm dosing off with the baby, I hear we out and that was it. I didn't think the nigga was in the basement piping the bitch down."

NuNu shook her head as he finished explaining the story.

"That nigga was bold as fuck," she said as she stood to grab her phone and send Leah a text.

"He is not allowed back over here Ty and I'm so far from playing." She stated.

"Enough said," he replied as he started talking to their son.

NuNu sent Leah a text asking if she was okay and waited for a response. She watched Ty as he doted over their baby. She was jealous and had no shame in voicing it.

"I hope I can get some attention when you finally put him down," she said, with a smug look on her face.

"You know I got you too baby," he said with a wink.

"My mom wasn't mad that you came and got him? She asked.

"Now you know Ms. Andrea was hotter than fish grease. She talked shit the whole time I was packing him up." He said with a chuckle.

Tyson laughed as he thought about all the shit she was talking. NuNu checked her phone to see if Leah had responded. *Dammit, Leah answer me*, she thought. She was worried about her and hoped she was okay. She couldn't believe Leah had taken off in her car, knowing damn well she could barely drive.

"I hope Leah is okay," NuNu stated.

"I'm sure she's good baby. Just give her a while, it's still early and she's probably still sleeping."

"Yeah, you're right. I'm hungry, you want breakfast?" she asked.

He nodded.

"Yeah, just make me whatever you want."

"Okay," she replied and headed to the kitchen to whip something up.

*L*eah got up the next morning feeling sick. She went over to her dresser, getting the pills her doctor had prescribed to her for nausea and took one chasing it with water. Stacy was gone for the weekend and Leah was home alone. NuNu and Marcus had been blowing her up all night after leaving NuNu's house. Her boss had called to check on her and while on the phone, Leah put in her request to go on maternity leave. Other than her boss she wasn't answering for anybody and just wanted to be left alone. Her life was a mess and she didn't know what to do to begin to clean it up. How she had allowed Marcus to cheat and lay hands on her was mind blowing.

She laid across her bed drowning in tears as she listened to Xscape *Run Around*. *If this fucking song isn't my life right now*, she thought herself. Her phone dinged and it was a text from Marcus telling her to come outside so they could talk. It was the same routine. He would fuck up and he would come back crying, hollering he's sorry. Leah was tired and had no energy for the back and forth. She was standing firm on her decision. They were done and she meant it. Leah ignored the text and went right back to her thoughts. She was depressed and if she was honest with herself, she was miserable. For months she only wanted to be left alone outside of going to school and work. She even spent her 19th birthday in her room not wanting to be bothered. The birth of her god baby was the only day she was genuinely happy, he had brought her so much happiness seeing his face that day. Whenever she was around Marcus, she faked happiness because he had told her that her walking around looking depressed all day damn wouldn't help her in any way. She just went with the motions as she tried her hardest not to argue with him so he wouldn't hit her.

Seemed like ever since the first time she forgave him it continued and just got worse. She went to work and school with make up on sometimes hiding bruises so no one would question her about it. How and why had she let this become her life? She was supposed to be experiencing the happiness that NuNu had. How did she end up enduring such trauma? These questions ran through her mind rapidly. Was it because of the things she experienced growing up that let her believe that the pain she endured was worth giving her child a family? She didn't have the answers, but she desperately yearned for them. Leah looked in the mirror and the person she saw staring back was not an image of herself. She heard glass break as she turned from the dresser and went into the hallway from her bedroom. *What the fuck?* She thought as she crept toward the front hearing a voice. She ran back to her room and grabbed her phone and proceeded to dial 911 until she felt a strong hand reach around her and snatched the phone. She spun around seeing Marcus standing there with blood dripping from his arm.

"What the fuck are you doing here?" Leah yelled looking at him in disgust.

"Naw, what the fuck is you doing not answering my fucking calls with your dumb ass?" He asked.

"Nigga fu-," was all she could get out

SMACK.

Leah hit the floor hard with tears in her eyes.

"Bitch you always got some slick shit to say!" Marcus barked.

Leah looked at him utterly confused. She couldn't believe he had the audacity to be laying hands on her, yet again after what she saw last night. She didn't understand how this could be turned around on her as if she was the offender. The longer she sat on the floor, the more her mind raced. She grew enraged. Leah refused to be Marcus's punching bag any longer. She wasn't about to keep enduring being beat on. Leah didn't care how much she wanted her daughter to have a real family. His physical abuse was not worth the family she wanted to provide. She would rather be a single mother than to deal with her woman beating, ass man. Marcus was not about to continue to endanger her or their unborn daughter.

Leah stood up, looked him square in the eyes. She dropped her head in despair and then held her arms out for him.

"I'm sorry Marcus," she said, voice barely audible.

Marcus smirked as he started to approach her. *She's weak for me,* he thought. Then a slight amount of guilt coursed through him. He started feeling bad for how he had just smacked her and now she was the one apologizing. Manipulation. Marcus thought he was manipulating Leah and he felt fucked up inside. Leah raised her head and spit directly in his face.

"Nigga, you got me fucked up if you thought I was about to let this shit ride," Leah yelled.

Marcus swiped a hand down his face and instantly grew heated. He stared at her, eyes blazing.

"You nasty bitch!" He barked.

Leah punched Marcus dead in the nose and kicked him right in the dick. He instantly dropped to his knees from the strong force behind the kick she had just delivered. She was about that life today. He would soon realize that she wasn't to be fucked with.

"Yeah nigga some of that," she spat.

Marcus hollered in pain as Leah stood there. She was tired of the bullshit. Leah had just caught him with a bitch the night before and here he was acting like shit was her fault. Marcus tried to get up, but Leah punched him so damn hard she busted his nose and blood instantly started dripping as he landed back on the floor. Leah hurriedly grabbed up her phone and rushed out of the house as she dialed 911. She locked herself in Stacy's truck as she waited for the police to arrive. She was a wreck and needed her best friend.

Leah: *Please come get me Nu*

My Nu: *On my way*

244

Leah cried as she heard sirens approaching. She stepped out as the officers approached the house.

"What's the issue, ma'am?" The officer asked as he scanned the scene.

"My child's father and I had a fight and he put his hands on me, I want him to leave," Leah cried.

The lady officer started asking questions as the other went into the house. Ten minutes later he walked out with Marcus cuffed and his head hanging down. Once they got close enough, he lifted his head turning to Leah.

"*BITCH!*" He said as he walked past with blood still seeping from his nose.

Leah shook her head. She didn't understand how he could be so disrespectful. Even though she should have been accustomed to his outburst of disrespect, his words always hurt the same as if it was the first time. She was his child's mother. He was supposed to be loving on her and protecting her. Hell protecting their child. But no, he was doing the complete opposite, causing physical harm to them and Leah was tired. She knew that had she not called the police that it probably could have gotten a lot worse. She was certain she had done the right thing by calling the police. The officer speaking with Leah finished taking her statement as Marcus was being put in the back of the patrol car, pulling away with him staring at her while shaking his head.

CHAPTER TWENTY

☐

2 months later

$\mathcal{L}$eah awoke in a hospital bed in so much pain. She hit her call button for the nurse to bring her pain medication. Looking to her right she saw NuNu in the chair burping her newborn daughter. Ma'Laysia Bre'Ana Hill had made her entrance into the world on May 21st after 17 hours of labor that resulted in an emergency c-section. Leah was at NuNu and Tyson's when she went into labor and had been rushed to the hospital in the back of an ambulance. She went through so much agony as she prepared to give birth to her daughter. Leah stopped dilating at 6 cm and being that her water had already broken she was prepped for a c-section to deliver her daughter before she had her first bowel movement which would harm her if she tried to eat it. The nurse walked in and asked Leah what she could do for her. Leah told her she was in pain and needed medicine so that she could hold her baby girl. Even the slightest movement brought tears to her eyes. She lay as still as possible as she looked over at NuNu and her baby.

"Leah, she looks just like you," NuNu said as she kissed the top of the hat that rested on Ma'Laysia's head.

Leah smiled. She hadn't got a chance to see her daughter after she was removed from her stomach because she kept getting sick. Leah wondered what she looked like the entire time until exhaustion took over.

"Thank god," she said, placing her hand on her forehead.

She had spent the last two months hating her daughter's father, that she was certain that she would come out looking like him. Leah hadn't spoken to Marcus since the day he broke out her god mother's window, coming in and putting his hands on her. She was in no mood to be in his presence. Their first court date after the incident she had requested a continuance until after the baby was born, blaming it on not wanting to be inside a courtroom in her current condition. The nurse walked back in, giving Leah a pill for the pain and a cup of water to wash it down with.

"Have you heard from Marcus?" NuNu asked as the nurse made her exit.

"No," Leah said, shaking her head as she leaned back against the pillow and wincing from the pain.

"Leah you're about to be pissed but he is on his way up here," NuNu stated.

"What do you mean he is on his way?" Leah said, rolling her eyes in NuNu's direction.

"I had Ty call him to tell him about Laysia," NuNu said as she stood and walked over to her and placed Ma'Laysia on her chest softly.

"Nu I didn't want that mufucka nowhere around me," Leah whispered.

"Leah he won't touch you in a hospital and regardless of the hate I have for his punk ass that's Laysia's dad," NuNu said.

Leah was pissed. If she wasn't in so much pain, she would have cussed NuNu out. She wasn't ready to see Marcus. If she had been, she would have placed the call herself. Stubborn. Leah was stubborn. She would have waited as long as she could before she called Marcus to tell him about their daughter being born.

The side effects of the medicine started to kick in and Leah felt her eyelids getting heavy. "Get Ma'Laysia for me Nu," Leah said as her eyes fluttered up and down. Since she had to have a c-section, she was prescribed to take both a Vicodin and Percocet which had Leah feeling like she was floating, the pain eased, and exhaustion took over her body.

Leah woke up to the sounds of multiple people. She never opened her eyes. She just laid there listening as she heard Marcus, his mama, NuNu and another voice she didn't recognize. She heard Marcus telling NuNu that his baby girl was too pretty and then his mama whispered asking him if he was sure the baby was his because she sort of looked Mexican. That pissed Leah off and she started to open her eyes and say something but NuNu was all over his mama's head about her and her goddaughter.

"Um, what you mean is he sure? Don't nobody want to trap your ugly ass son miss trust me," NuNu said snappishly. Marcus's voice cut in telling his mother to chill. Leah finally opened her eyes.

"Nu, please bring me my baby?" she asked as she lifted the head of her bed.

Marcus stood with his daughter and walked over to her and laid the baby on top of her chest gently.

"She looks just like you Leah," Marcus said as he rubbed his daughter's head softly.

Leah. Marcus hadn't called her that since the day they met. It sounded foreign like he was just meeting her for the first time today. He hadn't seen Leah since the day she put him in jail. She didn't show up for their court hearing and she never picked the phone up or responded to his messages.

Looking at her now did something to Marcus, she was gorgeous, and shame started fill him. Leah didn't respond. She just laid there caressing her baby's back. The doctor walked in and instructed that he needed everyone to clear the room so that he could examine Leah's incision. *Thank God*, Leah thought to herself. She was ready for everyone to leave Marcus and his messy ass mama particularly. Everyone made their rounds as they rubbed Ma'Laysia back including the voice she didn't recognize which turned out to be Marcus's younger sister, telling Leah that they would be back to visit the next day.

"Thank you for my baby girl Leah," Marcus said.

Again, Leah didn't utter a word back to him and he shook his head. She wasn't letting down her guard. Even with the birth of their baby, she was making sure her wall with him was solid. Had NuNu not called him, Leah was certain that she would not have picked the phone up to let him know about their daughter being born no time soon.

"Thanks for calling NuNu," he said and departed.

NuNu looked at Leah with empathy and then headed for the door as well. She knew her friend would be stubborn for a long while before she would consider speaking to Marcus again.

"I'll call you later," she said.

Leah nodded in response. She looked down the bridge of her nose at a sleeping Ma'Laysia and whispered, "I'm going to be better for you little love." Leah found her strength in her daughter. As much as she missed Marcus, dealing with a cheating and abusive ass nigga was no longer an option for her. Courage. Ma'Laysia was Leah's courage. She had given her mother the courage to walk away knowing that she needed to be the one to protect them both. Marcus had violated them and put them both in harms way with hitting on Leah. No matter what, Leah would look at her daughter knowing she made the right choices regarding their lives from this day forward.

5 months later

$\mathcal{L}$eah looked around the banquet hall at the decorations that she and her god mom had set up for her and NuNu's graduation party but also a surprise birthday party for NuNu. Tyson had spared nothing when it came to the party and wanted the girls to enjoy their day. Everyone was so proud of them. The girls still managed to walk across the stage that past June and NuNu got her wish to attend prom with Tyson in attendance. Stacy looked at Leah smiling and then embraced her. "I'm so proud of you Bre'Ana, you did it baby, you did it," she said as she took a step back taking in Leah's outfit. Leah wore an all black Apple Bottom Jean outfit with a silver shirt underneath and silver five-inch heels.

"All sucky-sucky," Stacy said to her god daughter as she circled her.

"My baby poppin' today," she said laughing with Leah.

"You so silly mama," she said as she walked over to Ms. Andrea and grabbed MaLaysia. "Hey LayLay," she said, calling her by the nickname NuNu had given her.

She hated it at first but NuNu refused to stop calling her by the name, so it eventually grew on her. Leah scooped her up and Ma'Laysia's smile warmed her entire heart.

"You for sure got your mommy smile," she told her, kissing her soft cheeks.

Ma'Laysia grabbed Leah by the face and put her mouth on her nose, wetting it up with her drool. Leah squealed as she wiped her nose.

"I guess you're giving out kisses on the nose today huh little love," she said as she gave her back to Ms. Andrea.

Leah turned the car seat that Little Tyson was sleeping in and bent down to kiss his cheek. The babies were growing so fast and the bond they had you would have thought they were blood brother and sister. Leah stood back up as she swept her bangs out of her face.

"Everyone is starting to pile in, what time did you tell Ty to bring Nu?"

"They should be here within 5 minutes," Ms. Andrea said as she bounced Ma'Laysia on her knee.

The DJ was starting to play tracks, kicking the party off with *Dilemma* by Nelly. Stacy was bringing out the last bit of food to set on the table. Leah was busy making her way around greeting her friends and others from school that were invited. Tyson had sent Leah a text telling her that they were about to come in. Leah got the mic from the DJ and instructed everyone to get quiet because the birthday girl was heading in. The doors of the hall opened and NuNu walked in looking gorgeous as ever. She wore a red Baby Phat spaghetti strapped dress that went a little past her knee and gold open toe six-inch heels.

Tyson had placed a mask over NuNu's face before they left the house. He led her into the center of the dance floor as she held one had on top his and the other out to the side trying to keep her balance. "Ty, it feels like I'm going to fall," she said smiling.

"I got you lor mama." He removed the mask and everyone in unison yelled *"surprise"* and started singing *Happy Birthday* by Stevie Wonder. NuNu was a ball of emotion as she smiled and wiped at her eyes. She turned to Tyson and he leaned down kissing her forehead.

"Ty, you're so good to me," she whispered in his ear.

"I'll always be good to you Nu'Asia, believe that."

Leah felt a tap on her shoulder and as she spun around, she anticipated seeing a face she didn't want to see. *I don't have time for this shit,* she thought as she turned to face the unwanted. To Leah's surprise, it was a face that she hadn't seen in 8 months. She looked the tall figure up and down taking him in. His *Hugo* cologne blessed her nostrils and she breathed deep wanting his scent to stay locked in. This man was the most handsome thing walking in Leah's eyes. How she didn't notice the first time she laid eyes on him blew her mind. He wore blue Tommy Hilfiger Jeans and a white Tommy Hilfiger polo, with a silver necklace dangling from his neck that held a cross on it. He had to be at least 6 feet because he towered over her making Leah feel like a dwarf even with the heels on.

"Hi," she said, eyes burning into his.

"Hi, *I'm Busy*," he shot back with a wink.

Leah couldn't contain her smile any longer as she dropped her head growing nervous, biting her bottom lip. She hadn't felt this way in a very long time and the feeling scared her.

"Don't be so tense," Jamison said, being able to read her body language as he caressed her cheek.

Leah looked up and they locked eyes.

"I told you I'd be seeing you again," he said softly.

"That you did," she whispered.

Leah's attention was snatched from Jamison when Dominic bumped into her. She turned on her heels and froze seeing his face. She hadn't thought about what happened in months and here was Dominic giving her a reminder.

"My fault Leah," Dominic said as he looked down at his phone confused.

"Dominic," she said lowly.

Flashes of the day Amanda died started playing back in her mind and a chill went through her body. Leah knew everyone was invited but she didn't think he would accept the open invitation. Dominic looked down at his phone as another text from an unknown contact came across his screen.

Unknown: *It wasn't an accident*

Leah noticed the bewildered look on his face and started to ask him what was wrong until the figure standing in the window staring directly at her caught her attention. Leah's eyes widened in shock. "No fucking way," she said.

To be continued in Betrayal 2

Thank you all for taking this journey with me as I step into the literature world. The love and support you all have shown throughout this journey means everything to me. Please, bare with me on this ride because it's going to be a bumpy one but yet will smooth out, it's only the beginning. I hope you all enjoyed the first book and will be anticipating the second just as well as I am anticipating writing it. Please if you are not a member in my book group, join us on FaceBook at Author A.Marie as we discuss your thoughts on the characters and book as well.

Questions

1. **Do you think Leah allowed Marcus to manipulate her because she wanted a family?**
2. **What do you think about the negative feelings NuNu has toward Marcus?**
3. **Tyson? Please give me all thoughts on Tyson. Is he as solid as he seems or is he just slick with his stuff and hasn't been caught yet?**
4. **Do you think Marcus mother plays a part in the way he treats Leah? They have a lot of discord**
5. **What are your thoughts on Leah's god mother Stacy? Could she have done more to nurture Leah?**
6. **What do y'all think about Dominic having a relationship with NuNu first but actually ended up falling in love with Mandy?**

7. **Do you think what happened to Mandy is Dominic's karma after realizing it was her he loved and then lost her?**

I want to give a special thanks to Bianca and B.Edits. B, you will never ever know how much you are appreciated. Our late nights and all of our back and forth was well needed and a very big lesson. From the bottom of my heart I thank you for believing in me and pushing me to be better in my writing. Much love sis… You are a real one!! My B…

Made in United States
North Haven, CT
19 November 2021

11280680R00157